Dates, Drugs

and *Disco*

A Nikki Rodriguez Mystery

By M.A. Hansen

I0680485

This book is a work of fiction. The characters, incidents, story, and dialog are drawn from the author's imagination. None of the characters are real. Any resemblance to actual events or living or dead persons is entirely coincidental.

Cover art is designed by Mariah Sinclair, <u>mariahsinclair.com</u>

Prologue

Evening arrived around 8:30 pm when the bright sun had set on Rancho Niguel. The late spring breeze swayed the golden palm trees outside against a purple midnight sky. Nurse Cabela walked to her car in the four-story parking garage at Rancho General Hospital.

Smiling and reminiscing to herself about her last patient Mr. Giacomo she recalled, he was such a tease, his charming gentle manner and the poetry that he recited every time she walked into his room were part of his unique personality.

He recently became her patient when he had his heart valve fixed. Forty-five years old and now healthier than when he first arrived. He owned and operated a trucking company called Giacomo Transportation, one of the largest in the area.

Italian-born and bred just like herself, Mr.Giacomo was special to Kristin, he was very handsome and tall with dark short hair and dark eyes, and he spoke Italian too!

The language he learned from his grandmother he told her one rainy afternoon. Kristin had fallen in love with him and even though he was ten years older than she was it didn't matter to her. He had complete admiration for her and she envisioned a wonderful future together. Today, they had taken lunch out on the patio of the hospital cafeteria. Even though the hospital subway sandwiches were flavorless, they enjoyed them, they laughed and had a great conversation. He even promised her a fancy dinner,

"One of my best friends Tony is the head chef at Kendle's Restaurant, he makes the best pasta dishes and Chicken Parmigiana, which my grandmother would be proud of." Mr. Giacomo told her.

She replied, "Well at least I can make the best cannolis this side of California..."

She slightly chuckled as she reached her new Toyota GR Supra in Nitro Yellow. She got a great deal from John Wayne Toyota and Subaru, from Jazz Montgomery, He was such a great salesman no pressure. It was so new she still had a temporary paper license plate on the back. Her car shined in the dim light, and she thought, I'll drive out to the beach this weekend and cruise PCH.

Maybe when Donnie heads home I'll ask him to go to Malibu with me. Mr. Giacomo insisted that she call him Donnie his first name. She knew he was a masterful businessman and hopefully, the rumors were not true about his affiliation with union bosses.

But Kristin didn't care she knew Donnie and she was 100% sure that he is a good man.

Kristin heard a noise and looked around but there was no one there. The hospital garage lay empty, flooded with dim fluorescent lighting. She knew better than to take her time walking to her car, especially with all of the current drama in her life.

 She silently criticized herself for being so negligent about her safety. The parking garage was empty and now silent, there was no one around and now she came to her senses and quickly went to her car.

She clicked her key fob and opened her door, she tossed her purse over to the passenger seat, and then just when she was about to get in, she felt something around her neck tightening, she tried to fight, to free herself, she kicked and pulled but it was no use. He had a tight grip on her neck, the thick rope felt like strong plastic or rubber, tighter it griped around her neck and then all that she saw was darkness as she faded away. Kristin fell to the floor, her last memory was of Donnie, and then there she lay next to her beautiful car..

Chapter 1

It's Not Good News

Finally, it's June and Summer is almost here! Little Black Dress was invited along with three other bands to sing at the Kick-off to Summer Festival at the Rancho Niguel Park and Gardens. A fun festival, with food booths and trucks, vendors selling flowers and gifts, a dog show, and a kid's relay race.

2:15 pm and twenty minutes until we go on stage, I went over our last-minute costumes. We all decided to go for a more family-friendly summer look, instead of our usual little black dresses. We selected matching light denim bootleg jeans,(more like slim bell bottoms) gingham halter tops, and matching heels. Each gal wore a different color, I wore red gingham, Roxy wore yellow, Dana in blue, Taylor in purple, and Emily in green. We looked so summery with a 1970s flair. The sun was high in the sky a nice 82 degrees but with all of the trees around us, the stage was in the shade. Thank you for that!

Our first song of the day, "Got To Be Real" By Cheryl Lynn

We had a full audience, a lot of people were dancing and clapping along with the music.

Sara, Matt's little sister, and her boyfriend Jagger waved to me from their table off to the side of us. I smiled and waved back to them.

"Hot Stuff" By the late and greatest of all Disco, ok just my opinion! Donna Summer was our next song. My eyes usually stay focused on my audience but I couldn't help to look over at the parked Firetrucks and the booth for the 909 fire station. Matt still wasn't speaking to me, even though it had been almost four months, since our fight over me keeping Sara's whereabouts from him. I thought he would come around but he still did his best to ignore me.

After our last song was over, we were done for the day. "Thank you, everyone." I waved and blew kisses. We exited the stage and I told the ladies I'd be right back to meet them for dinner at one of the many food trucks here. Roxy and the other girls took their bottled water and tried to find some open tables.

"Nikki, you were so awesome!" Sara said as she hugged me.

"You really jammed Miss Nikki." Jagger Sara's boyfriend said.

Sara's summer look took her back to her natural blond and now she sported some daisy dukes and a pink tank top, with some low-top Converse in pink. Her large falsie eyelashes stayed the same and her bright pink lipgloss shined like enamel.

7

"Ooh, I like the lipgloss that's pretty. So how is school? I haven't had a chance to talk to you in a week." I asked her.

"Everything is so perf!" She remarked, I guessed that "perf" meant perfect, uh this generation loves their made-up language.

"Jagger can you get me a Coke please." Sara batted her eyelashes innocently.

"Yeah babe, I'll be back" Jagger ran off.

"Ok, now we can talk." She said more matter of fact.

"About what?" I asked cluelessly.

"I need a job, do you think when Kendle's opens I can work for you?"

"Sure Sara, you know it's a done deal, but how does your brother feel about it?"

"He just said I needed to get a Summer Job, he didn't say where. School is out in two weeks and Kendle's is going to open in that time frame right?"

"I think you should at least tell him where you are working, I don't want him to accuse me of not telling him what is going on with you."

"Don't worry I'll square it away right now." She said full of excitement!

Jagger came back with her Coke and they fled off.

"We'll be right back Nikki." She waved.

I went off to find the girls. Oh, Sara, she was brewing something, what is she up to?

Our table was crowded with the band gals and most of my friends, Martin and Oliver, Jessica and Mrs. Green were there all sharing a very large plate of wings from The Flying Hog Wings and Drinks.

"Nikki, I have a drink waiting for you girly." Oliver said coming over to me.

"Thank you." I sat down and took a long drink of my peach-iced tea. I was so thirsty. I platted a few wings with cool ranch dressing and dug right in. The band on stage was singing a K.C. & the Sunshine Band song "Keep it Comin' Love."

Everyone was chatting and having a great time.

Sara and Jagger came back and joined our table for snacks. Soon we had some mini taquitos with guacamole, some mozzarella sticks with marinara, and a plate of pot stickers with a sweet chili sauce.

Sara whispered to me.

"Don't worry he knows, he wasn't happy about it but I told him if he didn't let me work for you I would call mom and tell her to come for a week-long visit."

I gave her a surprised look, and she laughed and sipped her Coke. Matt would have agreed to anything Sara was bargaining with to keep his mom away for a week.

Martin handed me a Blue Moon beer and some orange wedges.

"Thanks, I love these."

"I've just discovered them, I'm hooked aren't they good?" He asked.

"Oh yeah!" I remarked.

As I was taking a long swig of my beer, a familiar voice interrupted Mrs. Green's story about her recent trip to Key West.

"So Marge and I were about ready to go out and lay on the fabulous beach there while the guys went golfing when all of a sudden..."

"Mrs. Green I'm sorry to bother you but I need to speak with you."

He tapped her on the shoulder, she turned and saw Paul looking at her with his detective look, still and stern with concern.

"Ok, sure." Mrs. Green looked puzzled but walked a few feet from our table, Paul saw me but didn't say a word. He was telling Mrs. Green something when she teared up and yelled "Nikki!"

I ran to her, with everyone at our table watching and wondering what Paul told her.

Mrs. Green pulled me into her arms and sobbed. I looked at Paul over her shoulder and mouthed the words "What's going on?"

Paul took off his Oakley shades.

"A very close friend of hers was found murdered. She was the next of kin."

I rubbed Mrs. Green's back and held her while she sobbed! Somewhere a handkerchief came from someone.

Mrs. Green dried her eyes. "I just can't believe it, Kristin my friend has been murdered, she was like a niece to me, I knew her parents for so many years."

Mrs. Green broke down again, and Oliver came over and held her. Paul put his shades back on.

"I'm very sorry for your loss Mrs. Green, tomorrow if you can come by the station we can talk and go over some questions I have about Kristin."

Mrs. Green shook her head yes to respond to Paul.

Paul was very sweet, he rubbed Mrs. Green's arm and told her, "I'm sorry."

He turned and walked away but I wanted to know more, I wasn't done! I caught up to Paul. "Do you know how she was killed? Do you have any witnesses, Paul please give us more information."

He stopped and turned to me

"Nikki, this is an investigation leave the police work to the professionals."

I didn't want to get into anything here at the park but if he was referring to investigating a crime he sure didn't believe *me* when I told him I know his precious ex-girlfriend Stacie is the culprit behind the attempted murder of me and my car and the explosion at Kendle's back in February.

What was it going to take to make him see? Instead, I went for being nice!

"Please Paul this isn't about us, Mrs. Green is like family."

He stopped and looked at me. "Can you tell Mrs. Green to be at the station at 10 am tomorrow, thanks." With that, he walked away.

Chapter 2

We Don't Need Charlies Angels

When I was a kid I watched the reruns of a classic TV show called Charlie's Angeles. It was an Aaron Spelling show made in 1977, with actresses Jacklyn Smith, Farrah Faucet, and Kate Jackson.

Three beautiful gals, fresh from the police academy working as officers in Los Angeles. When one day a very rich man named Charlie hires them to work for his detective agency. I remember loving all of the action and the detecting these ladies would do.

I knew that when I grew up I would want to give people justice for the wrongs that were done to them, which is why I was pre-law in college. I turned on the TV and changed it to the local news, Chanel 5 had the story on from yesterday's grizzly discovery of the body of Kristin Cabela, Mrs. Greens' dear friend.

The reporter on the scene stood in front of the parking garage at Rancho General Hospital.

"Good morning, I have here with me Detective Craig Zane. Detective, can you give us the details of what happened here?"

The reporter asked standing next to a stoic Craig.

He stood tall with his hands at his sides, ready to give his report to the press.

"The victim Kristin Cabela a nurse, here at Rancho General was found by a few other medical personnel yesterday morning. We have word from the coroner that at this time her death is due to strangulation. We are asking that if anyone has any information at all or if they were a witness to the crime please contact the

Rancho Niguel Police Department.

The number is 555-0979 thank you."

He took a step back. The reporter continued to ask questions.

"Do you know if this is random or did she know who attacked her?"

"At this time we are still investigating."

This was all that Craig would say, he was trained to be vague with the facts of the case to the public, only so they could keep some evidence from the killer.

Craig took another step back, indicating he was done answering questions.

"Thank you, Detective Zane, now folks we will update you when the police have more information but at this time we are asking that if you saw anything suspicious in the hospital garage parking lot or if you saw the crime occur, then please contact the police. Once again we are

coming to you live from the parking garage at Rancho General

Hospital."

Just after the news report, my cell phone rang out to the song

"The Hustle" by Van McCoy.

"Hello."

"Nikki, I have a favor to ask of you."

Mrs. Green was on the line, she sounded a little worried.

"What can I do for you?"

"Oh Nikki, I hate to ask but do you think you can come with me to the

police station, I just don't think I can do this on my own, and after that,

I need to go to Kristin's place to pick up a few of her things."

"Of course Mrs. Green whatever you need."

"Oh, thank you, Nikki, I'm so grateful to you honestly I owe you one."

She said sounding relieved.

"Think nothing of it, Mrs. Green."

"Thank you, Nikki, I'll be downstairs at your place in fifteen minutes,

and thank you again, honey."

"Ok, no problem."

I decided to change from the sweats I had on to a pair of black slacks

and heels. I added a nice silk sleeveless blouse in light blue, and a

matching small purse in the same color. Mrs. Green arrived and we

went out to the jeep and drove to the station.

When we walked in Paul was already waiting in the lobby of the police department for us.

I don't know if it was disappointment or slight irritation on his face when he saw me walking in with Mrs. Green.

Knowing Paul it was probably a little of both.

"Good morning Detective Anderson, I think I'm ready."

A sad and forlorn Mrs. Green mustered up her courage to answer Paul's questions.

"Thank you for coming in Mrs. Green, I know it's difficult."

"Nikki," he just said and walked in front of me with Mrs. Green, oh boy, this should be interesting, I thought to myself.

The office was busy with detectives working and tapping away at computers or discussing cases.

Paul led us to a small boardroom or large office, take your pick. A long boardroom table in pine wood sat with six chairs around it. The bright lighting and the sunshine from the three large windows provided a mix of warm strong light in the room and it reminded me of a business boardroom. I was grateful to Paul at least we weren't having this conversation in a room they use for suspects.

I took a seat next to Mrs. Green and Paul sat across from us. He had a file with him and he had a plastic evidence bag filled with Kristin's black Coach handbag, her key fob, and a wallet.

Paul opened a large black notebook and began to write down some things.

"Would you like some water or a cup of coffee?" Paul offered.

"A glass of water please." Mrs. Green replied.

"Nikki, how about you?"

"Nothing, thank you."

Paul went out and came back with a cold bottle of Fiji water and a glass. He opened it and poured it into the glass and handed it to Mrs. Green.

"Here you are."

"Thank you, Paul."

He sat back down and opened his file, "First I need to know a few things about Kristin, such as does she have any other family?"

Mrs. Green stared at the evidence bag with Kristin's purse, she fought back tears, and then through a kind of emotional fog she spoke.

"Kristin's parents, they were very good friends of mine for many, many years, and they died in a car crash about five years ago." She took a sip of water and then continued.

"Kristin doesn't have any siblings but she does have some family back East in Connecticut. An Uncle and three cousins, but they aren't very close, she saw them once every couple of years. I was her only family close by."

"Now do you know if Kristin was seeing anyone?"

Mrs. Green wiped her damp eyes with a white handkerchief, she was feeling overwhelmed and sad now.

"Yes, she called me last week, she told me she met the most wonderful man, he's one of her patients. His name is Donnie Giacomo, she was his nurse. Usually, we have patients that flirt with the nurses or ask them out, and Kristin always had admirers she was a very pretty gal. We sometimes took lunch together when I worked there, she always knew the hospital gossip before it hit the nurse's station, she was very observant."

Paul was writing down what Mrs. Green was telling him, and he asked her about Kristin's co-workers and any other friends she had.

"She had a lot of friends everyone loved her, her co-workers trusted her, and she even gained the respect of some the most hot-headed doctors at Rancho General."

"So you don't think she had any enemies? Did she mention anyone following her or maybe did she see anything that would give her cause to feel that someone might be after her."

Mrs. Green thought hard she turned over some information in her head and responded with: "She did call me the other night and asked me to meet her for coffee. Today would have been our coffee date." Mrs. Green wept quietly then spoke again.

"She just told me that she had some news that was it, I assumed it was about her and Donnie."

Paul got a call on his phone. "Excuse me one second."

"Anderson." He answered.

"Ok, that's interesting, ok thanks." He hung up his phone and put it away in his back pocket.

"Is there anything new?" I asked Paul.

"A possible clue."

He was being vague just like Craig had been with the reporter, but I wasn't a reporter. So I politely demanded to know!

"Well, what is it?" I asked antsy to know what it was!

Paul varied whether he wanted to share but he then came out with it.

"The autopsy showed an imprint on Kristin's neck, the coroner said it looks like the letter L, it's toward the side of the neck. If you are having an open casket it would be visible."

Mrs. Green took a breath, "I haven't even thought about that yet."

I rubbed Mrs. Greens' back, "Do you have any more questions this has been very hard on her."

"I know." Paul looked at Mrs. Green sympathetically.

"Paul, do you have a motive yet? Do you have the time of death? Do you have any suspects in mind?"

"Nikki, please, we don't have much right now!" Paul seemed irritated.

"Paul at least we know it wasn't a carjacking or even a robbery, this had to be personal."

He ignored my assessment of the crime and directed his words to Mrs. Green.

"If I have any more questions I'll contact you." He stood up, he handed Mrs. Green the contents of the evidence bag. "These are Kristin's things, you can take them with you."

Mrs. Green took the bag "Thank you, Paul."

He opened the door for us and told Mrs. Green they would release Kristin in a few days and that if she needed anything to call him.

On our way back to the lobby Detective Sonya Smith came to speak with Mrs. Green.

"Mrs. Green, how are you doing?" She held her hand and sympathized with her.

While they were chatting I pulled Paul aside.

"Please tell me you have more than what you told us!"

"Nikki, even if I did I can't tell you anything, and I don't want you going behind my back and investigating, I don't need Charlie's Angels going around and compromising my investigation. Stay away from it."

His words cut like a saw, his breath heavy and heated on my neck.

As much as I wanted to hate him right now I didn't! He had on that really good-smelling cologne, why was I still so head over heels for this man?

"Nikki, can I speak with you?" Sonya asked now looking over to me.

"Sure, Detective Smith."

"We'll be just a moment." Sonya said ushering me to her desk on the other side of the room. I had a seat across from her.

"Nikki, do you remember when I told you we had more news about your attacker, well we got the shoe molds back from the lab and it looks like the perp wears a size 7 1/2 women's size which is the most common shoe size around. I don't know if that narrows it down but that's what we're looking at right now. We found female DNA at the scene and as far as whom it belongs to that's still in processing we are a little behind here now with the Murder of Kristin Cabela, the chief is going to pull all of us into the investigation, and it seems the mayor wants this wrapped up, and soon."

"Sonya, I think the person behind this is Stacie McDaniels she hates me, I just know it's her."

"I heard about some of her little shenanigans at Kendle's from Craig, and I've seen her around here, she's always hanging on Paul and fussing over him." Sonya looked disgusted by Stacies behavior

"You are right Sonya."

"I'll tell you what Nikki, I'll do some checking on a few things and I'll be in touch, ok."

"Thank you, Detective."

I shook her hand and went back to find Mrs. Green,

Paul was standing by the door to the lobby.

"Nikki," Paul was going to say something but I beat him to the punch, we were out of earshot of any listeners, so I whispered

"Charlie's Angels always solved the case."

I walked out to the lobby where Mrs. Green was waiting. Paul stood in the doorway, he pinched the bridge of his nose, his tell for being tired or frustrated, and closed the door.

Chapter 3

A Clue

After our meeting at the department, Mrs. Green wanted to go to Kristin's apartment. So we headed a few miles down the road to the large white stucco building called The Vineyards at Rancho Niguel. New and snazzy one and two-bedroom apartments, with walk-in closets, stainless steel appliances, full-size washers and dryers, and central air.

We drove into the gated community using a gate remote we found in Kristin's purse.

We drove around a few buildings, G, H and then we arrived at building J. We parked in a visitor's spot just beside the large pool and spa area. A few residents were sunning on the lounge chairs and a few were taking a dip to cool off in the 82-degree heat.

The place was fancy and the residents seemed like high earners, based on the variety of cars in the parking lot.

BMWs, large trucks, sports cars, Audis, and some high-end SUVs.

We walked through the corridor that led to a cobblestone court, with benches and a soft soothing fountain.

"It's right up here." Mrs. Green led me to an arched door, with three steps leading up to it.

She opened the door and we went into a one-bedroom apartment.

It was really cute, it reminded me of the old-fashioned apartments you see in the nice part of LA. Cute Spanish-style arches, and tiled fireplaces.

Mrs. Green put Kristin's items on the small wooden table in the tiny dining area.

"I'm going to get her favorite dress and shoes, maybe you could search for some clues?" She asked.

"Of course, I'm sure the police have been here but, let's see if they missed something."

Mrs. Green went off to the closet and I looked around the living room. I checked the drawers on a small desk behind the sofa. Nothing turned up just the usual desk items, pens, pencils, stapler, and tape, nothing unusual there.

I did see some flyers for LINKED TO YOUR HEART. The new dating service in town and I thought, if she was involved with Donnie Giacomo why would she keep flyers for a dating service?

It looked like the kind of brochure they mail out to all residents, an advertisement the size of a birthday card with colorful photos of happy couples claiming they had their wishes fulfilled by meeting their soulmate all through LINKED TO THE HEART!

I put it aside on the dining table and continued to search. I looked through the kitchen drawers nothing to be found there, it was a slim shot anyway.

Next, I went to the bathroom and searched some of the drawers in the vanity under the sink.

A hair dryer, a curling iron, a flat iron, Kotex, rollers, hair brushes, and a bag of cotton balls, all kept in cloth box organizers, as I pulled out the items I noticed a small black paper handle bag, it looked like a small gift bag one gets when they buy a small item from a boutique.

"What is this?" I pulled out a pink shower cap. I chuckled, why would she put a shower cap in here?

Then I noticed inside the gathers of the shower cap a flash drive was inside.

The flash drive looked like a small rubber sandal in hot pink, it also had a silver keychain on it. I stuffed the shower cap back in the bag and put the storage containers with the hair brushes and dryers back under the sink.

I put the flash drive in my pocket and went to find Mrs. Green she was selecting some jewelry from Kristin's glass jewelry box.

"Mrs. Green, did Kristin have a computer?"

"Yes, there should be a black laptop on her desk."

I walked back out of the room to the desk in the living room, there was no laptop there on the desk!

"Maybe the police took it because it's missing." I shouted out.

Mrs. Green came up behind me.

"That's a funny thing, I also noticed her Tiffany's silver key pendant necklace is missing, it was coupled with a heart, (Return to Tiffany's pendent) her mother wore the heart, and her mother was buried with it and Kristin wore the key around her neck she always had it on!"

We searched the evidence bags again and pulled all of the contents out of Kristin's purse and wallet but no necklace or pendant.

"You should tell Paul that it's missing, I think the killer might have taken it."

Chapter 4

The Hustle

After Mrs. Green went back up to her condo via the elevator, I took the stairs up to the third floor, to find Craig.

Kiana answered the door, "Hi, I hate to bother you but is Craig home?"

"Hey Nikki, he's still at work, I guess he has a new lead on the case because he said he would be unreachable and two hours late for dinner."

"Oh, I'm sorry to hear that but can you ask him to call me when he gets home it has to do with the case."

"Oh, it's so sad to hear about Kristin! Mrs. Green introduced me to her a few months back and she was a big customer of mine. I was so shocked to hear about her. Isn't it a tragedy?"

"Yes, I'll say, I went with Mrs. Green to the police department today Paul had some questions for her." I gave her my look of routine police questioning you know what I mean.

"Oh my gosh, well bless you for being by her side, you're a true friend Nikki."

"Thanks, well I better get going."

"Ok, Nikki and I'll give Craig the message as soon as he gets home."

"Thanks, Kiana."

I went back downstairs to my place and decided to see what was on this device from Kristin's apartment. It had to be important if it was hidden the way it was. As soon as I got to my door Roxy was waiting for me.

"I'm glad you're home, I have to talk to you," Roxy said.

We went inside and I grabbed two Cokes out of the fridge for us, "Ok what's up Roxy?"

"Ok, so I noticed you have been moody and down and I'm worried about you, you haven't dated in four months since Paul dumped you and Matt ended your friendship." Just then my doorbell rang and it was Jessica. I let her in and handed her a Coke too!

"Okay, so what's this all about you two?" I asked with some skepticism.

Jessica spoke next, "Nikki, you need to move on! Mr. Wonderful 1 and 2 are not coming back to you, I'm sorry I'm being a total jerk but this is an intervention, Roxy and I are worried that you're stuck in neutral and if you don't make a move you won't get passed that."

"Guys I'm fine, really! I just don't feel like going out with anyone, my heart is still raw." I sat on the sofa and put my hands on the side of my face in frustration. "I have moved on, but I just don't have any desire to date anyone."

Roxy came over and sat beside me "Look Nikki, I think it's time to forget about the past, Jessica and I have noticed how many times you have dodged going out with us."

"That's because you two tried to set me up on a date. I'm not comfortable with that, and I know you guys are just trying to help but I'm just not interested." I told them feeling confident with my choice.

Jessica and Roxy looked at one another deflated!

I went to the fridge, pulled out a lemon meringue pie, and set out some plates.

Jessica and Roxy walked over to me "Girl listen to me and don't be mad promise, I'm your bestie."

She hugged me to disguise her evil plot.

"I'm not mad at you two, really!" I said with sincerity, little did I know what was coming for me.

"Well, that might change." Jessica pipped in while taking a sample of the meringue and licking it off her finger.

"What are you guys talking about?"

I was on the edge now, something was a miss and my besties were in on it.

"See, we kinda..." Roxy trailed off and looked in the other direction, not wanting to look me in the eyes.

"What did you two do?" I asked now raising my voice an octave!

"Roxy signed you up for LINKED TO THE HEART, and your first-speed dating session is tonight at 7 pm at the Hampton Rancho Niguel."

Jessica spilled! She took a breath after she was done speaking, and looked like the kid that got caught in the cookie jar.

For me my head was ready to explode from the shock of being set up to go on a speed dating service, one that has been the talk of the town lately.

"I can't believe you two, Roxy what were you thinking?"

I swatted her on the arm!

"Look, I just thought you might need it since Paul and Stacie got back together and they have been seen out and about!"

Roxy said the word *together* slowly and apprehensively.

I mulled this over, *Paul went back to Stacie?*

My gut wrenched and I had this feeling of disappointment, maybe it was time for me to stop sulking and move on. I will always care deeply for Paul, but if he moved on, maybe I should too.

I'm sure he was tired of my non-commitment issues, who wouldn't be and why would anyone want to wait for someone to make a choice when it should come naturally?

Love was love and I should know by now who has my heart.

It also didn't help that Matt hated me too, Nikki, it's time to move forward. I accepted what they were saying, even though I just got hustled here.

"Ok, what do I have to do!"

Chapter 5

The Dating Game

I had about two hours until the final count down and then I was expected at the door at 7 pm to be a part of the new match-making service LINKED TO THE HEART! Part of me wanted to bail, except for the fact that Roxy confirmed that I would be there.

I couldn't destroy my rep, now with the success of the Youth Center and with Kendle's going back up, I didn't want to put a wrinkle in my word. I also felt that I needed to move on!

Roxy and Jessica had me get dressed up, they said to dress for a dinner date.

We combed through my closet and came up with my black halter midi dress in chiffon from White House Black Market.

I chose my black Dior heels and matching purse, I added my gold olive leaf cuff bracelet, and gold hoops, perfect!

By 6:45 pm I was ready to go.

I arrived at the Hampton at 6:55 pm and walked into the lobby, it was full of bachelors and bachelorettes, all heading to the grand ballroom.

The front double doors were open and a desk sat to the right of the entrance, where two young women sat with a laptop.

"Please form two lines, one for bachelors on one side, you will check in with Letty and bachelorettes will check in with me, I'm Tory."

We all followed her instructions and formed two lines, after checking my name off, Tory smiled a big bright smile, "Let me just say I'm a fan Ms. Rodriguez I love your music, will Kendle's be up and running soon?"

"It should just be a few weeks."

She put her hand to her chest relieved "Oh I'm so glad. Have a nice time in the game and good luck."

"Thank you, Tory."

I walked into the room and was directed to a table with two chairs, and a notepad, I sat down to wait for further instructions. Once every table was filled with two people, we got started.

There was a big drum roll, and then a woman dressed in a fuchsia suit came out.

"Hello, everyone I am CeeCee Sass, I am the owner of LINKED TO YOUR HEART, and I would just like to welcome y'all out here today, I'm going to hook you up." She laughed a large laugh with a big smile.

"Ok, so the object of this game is not only for you ladies to find a great man but to have fun while you are searching for y'all soul mates. First thing ladies, you have a gentleman in front of you, the object is to strike up a conversation and feel him out!

See if you have any sparks, you have three minutes and then we rotate and someone new sits in the chair and you converse with them and so forth for the next two hours.

Now at the end of the evening If you both agree to a date, come up to the front of the room and wait for your instructions for your first date. Then you go on your date and you come back here and tell us how it went. That's when we go live on our Pod Cast and the listeners call in and vote on where to send you on a date.

If that goes well you make it to the diamond date level and that's where it gets fun, and you continue until you make it to the Platinum level then you have found yo soul mate"

She laughed again "And don't forget CeeCee is invited to the wedding y'all! So let's get started!" She shouted with enthusiasm.

In front of me sat a nice guy, a history teacher over at Rancho Niguel high school.

He seemed nice enough and I thought maybe a date would work for us.

"I'm a big fan of yours, you run the Youth Center, bravo, I think it's a great addition to our community, I have several students that attend classes there."

"Thank you, I'm very proud of it."

He was cute, a nice boy next door type, with hazel eyes and light brown hair. He seemed easy to talk to. We shook hands and I put a star by his name on my scorecard.

The next guy wasn't my type, he had on an expensive suit and claimed to drive a Ferrari.

"So I'm in business for myself, I own a tech company in Pasadena, and I have many stocks, my portfolio is looking good, I have a big house in the hills and you would look wonderful on my arm, did I mention I have a Ferrari?" He winked.

Ugg next, please!

The next guy asked me what house I was in, he went on and on about Dungeons and Dragon and Harry Potter and The Game of Thrones, I had no idea what he was talking about. My eyes simply glazed over and I focussed on his long sideburns, with a touch of some silver, and the way the shape of them resembled a slender pork chop.

After the bell rang we switched and a new bachelor sat down.

"Jazz what are you doing here?"

"Looking for love too!"

My Salesman that sold me my Jeep, Jazz Montgomery, was also a fan of Little Black Dress.

He asked about my Jeep and if I was happy with it, I told him yes I'm head over heels for it. Jazz and I hit it off but we seemed more like good friends, it also didn't hurt that he reminded me of Shemar Moore, who is extremely handsome.

"I have to admit something, Nikki, I think I hit it off with Denise back there, she seemed to have a lot in common with me."

"Oh, Jazz ask her out for a date, if you feel she's the one don't wait."

He smiled and said

"I will, I guess I just needed a second opinion."

"I'm rooting for you let me know what happens?"

Our timer went off and Jazz moved to the next table. My third bachelor was a sports agent, he kept going on and on about whom he represented and how much the endorsements were, and how much he made last year.

After about 20 seconds I tuned him out, I casually scanned the room, to see how others were faring.

Then the timer rang and CeeCee shouted "Switch." I rolled my eyes and thanked God it was almost over. This evening seemed like a bust and I would have to let Roxy and Jessica know that I wouldn't be coming back for another round of this humiliation.

Before I was ready to throw in the towel and give up, my next bachelor a strikingly handsome dude approached my table.

I was stunned and hoping like hell my mouth wasn't hanging open with drool coming out, WOW! I was in complete approval now!

This was all I could think of at this point and I hoped that he had a great and interesting personality to go with the looks!

Tall and very good-looking, athletic, and with nice strong arms, dark blue eyes, and dark hair, another Superman type! What is it with me and Superman?

He shook my hand, with a firm but polite grip! Confidence is what I felt.

"Hello."

"Hi." I smiled "I'm Nikki Rodriguez." I managed to squeak out.

"My name is Nicolas Williams III, everyone calls me Nick."

"Great name, you're already earning points with me."

I replied.

"Well Nikki, you look stunning this evening."

"Thank you, Nick, you're looking pretty stunning yourself."

I looked into those midnight blues and wondered what was there behind them, what did he do for a living? What were his hobbies? Where was he from? I hadn't seen him in the area.

"So tell me what do you do for a living?" He asked.

"I am in a band Little Black Dress, we are local here and I own a few businesses in town, Kendle's Restaurant, and Bella Rancho Realty."

"I've been to Kendle's a few times, the food is wonderful, wow I'm impressed." He smiled.

"What about you, what's the daily grind?" I asked him smiling.

"I'm a Cardiac Surgeon at Rancho General Hospital. "

A surgeon wow, so let me see I placed him at maybe 33-36 years of age.

"A surgeon wow! That's quite a career. You're at Rancho General then you must know my good friend who just retired from there GG Green or as we all call her Mrs. Green."

"Oh yeah everyone knows Mrs. Green, she was a hell of a nurse, I heard she retired about six months ago."

"Yes, so tell me what do you like to do in your spare time, you know hobbies and such." For some reason, my smile was plastered on my face and the butterflies in my stomach were driving me crazy.

"I like to ski and hike, do some fishing, and I just started this it's my new favorite sport, I recently started surfing." He looked excited to discuss surfing.

"I ski and I surf too, wow, I started surfing last year when my bo... my friends taught me."

I had almost slipped up and said, boyfriend.

We discussed his new adventure and our ages he's 35 and I told him my age I will be 30 in a few months.

I told him about owning Kendle's, my position at the Youth center, and my band. We quickly chatted about which beach was best for the waves, and before we knew it the bell rang.

CeeCee yelled again "Switch"

Nick was slow to get up but he asked me if I would accompany him at the end of the evening to the front of the room."

"Yes, of course."

He moved to the next table but kept looking over at me, we locked eyes a few times and finally at the end of the night, CeeCee master of ceremonies closed the game.

"Ok, fellas all of you that had a connection come up here, form a line."

Ten bachelors walked to the front of the room and stood side by side. CeeCee walked up to Bachelor One, he selected his date, and next Jazz selected Denise and she came up to stand with him, the next Bachelor selected his match and fourth was Nick, and he asked: "Nikki would you like to accompany me on a date?"

I smiled and replied "Yes" I walked up to stand beside him.

When all of the bachelors were paired up there were six couples upfront. CeeCee congratulated us and then gave her speech.

"Ok, ladies and gentlemen, these six couples have consented to a first date, let's give them a hand, and for those of you who didn't find a match tonight, you can come back tomorrow and try again.

"See you next time folks and remember you can be matched by LINKED TO YOUR HEART."

The room began to clear out for the other bachelors and bachelorettes but the last six couples, we followed Tory to the back of the room where she had a basket filled with red envelopes.

"Ok men, pick an envelope and it will tell you where you and your date will be going."

Jazz was first and his date destination was: a limo chauffeured ride to Arrowwood Mountain Resort in Lake Crestline, for a canoe ride in the lake, and dinner at the resort.

Next was Nick's turn, he selected an envelope and it read "Begin your date on Saturday afternoon with a hot air balloon ride to the Rancho Vista Winery for dinner."

"That sounds like fun, I can't wait." I smiled again.

We left the hotel ballroom and Nick walked me to my car, he asked me why I decided to sign up for LINKED TO YOUR HEART.

"My best friend signed me up and she told me about it... Oh, two hours ago."

"Oh no not you too!" He chuckled.

"Your friends hooked you up to do this too!"

I asked him.

"Oh yeah, a bro of mine at the hospital, Dr. Ferguson, we went to college together at UCLA, he said Nick It's time you stop living at the hospital and meet someone that doesn't need heart surgery."

We both laughed.

"Well, I guess they know something we don't, right."

"Yeah, that's true."

"This is me." I stood in front of my red Jeep.

"Adventure girl, I like it, a Jeep! I have an old Toyota Tundra for my recreation hobbies like my surfboards when I surf but this is cool!"

He was checking out my new wheels.

"I just recently purchased it, and I'm loving it."

"This is me right here." Nick said as he walked two cars away

"Whoa, nice, this is yours?"

I said looking over the vehicle.

"Yes, this is the daily."

Parked in front of me was the most beautiful Chevy Convertible Corvette Z06 in Rapid Blue, American muscle cars were awesome and right now I was in car heaven.

"I love the car, wow, how fast does it go?"

"You'll have to find out on Saturday." He smiled.

"I'm looking forward to it!"

I got in my Jeep, waved to him, and headed home.

Chapter 6

Move n' On Up

When I got home I got into my jammies and checked my phone for messages. I had a call and a message from Craig, he asked me to call him back when I had a chance. It was 10 pm so I sent him a text message.

Hi Craig,

Sorry I wasn't available for your call

But I was ambushed by my two buds

And I had a date with LINKED to the Heart

The new dating service. Not by choice.

So if you can come by tomorrow I think I have

Some information on your case.

Thanks

Nikki

I guess he was up because he responded right away

Ha, Ha, I heard about that! I stopped at Stellas Coffee Shop to get an apple pie and I spotted Roxy and Jessica, I asked them where you were and they told me. Sorry to hear you got suckered! I'll come by tomorrow morning at 8 am.

I gave a thumbs-up emoji and went to my Apple IMAC. I took out the sandal thumb drive and plugged it into the computer.

The files were mostly photos, but then I saw two videos, I clicked on one of them, but it was a grainy video, with low audio of someone in a white coat in a locker room.

You couldn't see a face because the video was taken on a slant as if someone set their phone to record but the phone fell sideways.

The quality of the video looked like there was limited reception so it, cut out twice and it was very difficult to see what was going on. Plus a locker door covered most of the person's body so you only saw the lower half of a person.

I heard what sounded like someone snorting something. Maybe cocaine, the mystery person is seen putting an item back in a locker. The video was maybe 10 seconds and then it ended.

I clicked on the other video, it had Kristin herself whispering from the same place in the locker room where she recorded the other video. She looked tired and her words were barely above a whisper.

"I just caught him again! He snorted some coke and he usually does this when he has a long shift at work or surgery.

43

I'm going to report him to the medical board! I confronted him

yesterday and told him what I saw. He denied it and said I was crazy.

He said if I didn't drop this allegation, he said I would be sorry!"

The video cut out too! It was very grainy and every other word carried static to it. I decided to hand it over to Craig tomorrow and tell him we found it on the floor by Kristin's dresser.

The next morning I got up early and got dressed, I was going to the construction site at Kendle's today. The new building was almost done and I had my decorator meeting me at 10 am.

Craig was punctual he was here right at 8 am. A light knock on the door and a view through the ring cam showed him patiently waiting, I opened the door.

"Hi Nikki, so what's this about?" He asked looking skeptical!

I let him in and then poured him a cup of coffee and offered him a slice of banana bread.

"Oh, thanks." He pleasantly replied sitting at the island kitchen counter.

"It's about this, Mrs. Green and I found it yesterday on the floor by Kristin's dresser, it must have fallen out of her drawer when you guys searched her place."

I held up the pink flash drive in the shape of a sandal, I dropped it in his hand.

"There are two videos on this drive but they are very grainy. I think Kristin had a confrontation with her killer the day before she died because the date of the videos is one day before her death."

"Can I use your computer?"

"Yes," I led Craig to the computer and he plugged in the flash drive. He watched the same two videos I saw last night. He said the same thing I did. "The video is pretty distressed I can't make out a face of the person she's accusing. Maybe tech forensics can work on this and try to get a better resolution of the video. This is good stuff Nikki, thank you."

"I want the killer caught."

After Craig left, I headed out for my meeting. I had the hard top of my Jeep taken off a few weeks ago and converted to the soft top, but today it was so nice I removed my soft top and went to a complete convertible.

I put a Dodgers ball cap on my head to keep my hair from flying in my face and turned on the tunes to some 70s mix.

The new building was just about done, when I arrived my contractor Sam came to give me the update.

"Nikki, good to see you, we have everything done, we had the inspector come and give us the thumbs up!"

He smiled.

We were inside touring the new restaurant, it was gorgeous!

The decorator arrived and she began to direct her employees to bring in the furniture.

The outdoor patio with the fountains and fire pit were running as several workers were testing them. The new place had more windows and a sliding glass wall that opened up to the patio seating.

I added a bar outside and one inside for faster beverage service and because it looked cool. It was modern and beachy! Sam and I went upstairs to view another area for outdoor and indoor seating. Umbrellas in yellow were up and now patio tables were being set out.

Next, we headed to the new banquet room off to the side of the building. One glass wall faced the garden with a man-made small waterfall that ran into a small lake, maybe more like the size of a small pool. It was gorgeous what can I say!

The flowers and plants were being planted in planters and large Spanish-style clay pots in white, they were put in corners where color was needed.

The banquet room was beautiful too! I went for an extra large room with, a high ceiling and wall to wall with hardwood floors. I had a large staircase put in, a very grand one with black Iron filigree posts and grades. It flowed up to a large terrace. A downstairs patio was also put in to access the view of the waterfall. For the walls, I decided on a smooth white stucco with wood beams on the ceiling.

It was a cross-between, a Spanish-style casa, and a beach house, a California staple.

Everything was looking good and with just one more week we would be ready to start training some new employees. Our Grand opening was set for July 1st.

In just one week and a half, the band would officially be rehearsing here in that time frame too!

We walked back down to the kitchen, it was a much larger one with more room for prep and for catering our events in the banquet room.

We added a locker room with two washrooms for male and female employees, we added a small lounge for meals, some new offices for Chef Stark, and the banquet manager, and one big office for Daisy and Tito as well.

My office was upstairs again but this time I put in my own loft, with a separate entrance as well as the general staircase that came from the back of the kitchen.

Two ways to get in, plus I added a nice bathroom, complete with a shower, and another small room with a twin bed and a dresser, and a small closet for late nights when I'm here for 14 plus hours.

The office decor followed the same beach theme, as the restaurant with, creams, white, and a few touches of pink instead of blue.

I decided on natural light wood for my desk to match the wood beams on the ceiling, it was very coastal looking. My lobby was much like the last time with white Pottery Barn sofas and a driftwood and glass coffee table.

I heard a loud laugh coming from downstairs and I knew Mayor CJ Groves was here.

I ran down the stairs and saw her talking to Sam my contractor, in the kitchen. Stacie McDaniels was right by her side smiling like the evil villain that she is!

"Mayor CJ how nice of you to stop by," I said with a fake smile plastered to my face.

"Oh, I was just commenting on how beautiful this place looks, Wow! It's Wonderful!" She said stretching out the word wonderful as she usually does. Stacie rolled her eyes behind the mayor, no doubt this was her Achilles heel!

"I won't keep you, I know you have a lot of work to do, but I just wanted to see the amazing progress."

"We're almost done and we will be re-opening in a week and a half. The grand opening will be big I promise." I told her.

"I can't wait! This place is movin' on up" She said enthusiastically.

"CJ, you have a 12-noon lunch that we need to get you to, and I have a lunch date with Paul." Stacie looked directly at me when she said this smiling like a wicked demon!

"That's right I do need to get to another engagement. I want to say thank you again for letting us come on in and see how it's going." She waved bye and so did Stacie with her red horns coming out from her head!

After they left I realized how hungry I was too! I went to tell Sam I was going to get lunch and if he or the others wanted anything. Sam and his crew were having their lunch in the garden area on the grass, one of his employees had his tablet on and they were sitting around watching the Jeffersons. An iconic comedy about a family that moves to the east side, business owners, now living in a deluxe apartment in the sky in New York City. I watched it too as a kid and loved Florence she was my favorite character the Jeffersons' housekeeper with sass and good comebacks for her boss.

I took another look at the new and improved Kendle's and in the words of George Jefferson, I said to myself we were "Move n' on Up!" I smiled and headed out.

Chapter 7

Strut

I walked into Sprouts Market and immediately went to the deli, I ordered a mozzarella, pesto, and tomato sandwich with a side of macaroni salad.

"Ok just give me about ten minutes we're a little backed up today." The young deli gal told me looking at the line that had formed behind me.

"Ok, I'll be shopping around." I replied.

The song "Forget Me Nots" By Patrice Rushen played over the speaker. Funny I was hearing disco music everywhere I went. It was fine by me I usually listened to all genres of music because we played all kinds of music in the band.

My second stop was to produce, I added some blueberries, and strawberries to my basket and some oranges, and a few cherries, (Rainier's are my favorite). Just then and before I had the chance to add some peaches, a little kid ran past me pushing his grocery basket with full force, I moved out of the way just in time before the little terror had the chance to strike me with it. As luck would have it I backed into someone coming around from the lettuce cooler.

"Oh, I'm so sorry, this little guy just came out of nowhere." I turned to see two big bright blue eyes staring at me.

Matt had his small basket in his right hand, he didn't smile he just said, "Don't worry about it."

He walked away, never looking back.

Are you kidding me? I was getting so tired of this treatment and it was just downright ridiculous.

I had been moping and feeling sad because of the fallout from my relationship with him, but it seemed like his anger for me was just as strong as four months ago. How much more sad XM could I possibly listen to?

Nikki just let him go, girl! He doesn't want your friendship anymore, you guys are through! Just walk away! My conscience fed me.

No! Don't let him off that easy, give him a piece of your mind. He has it coming for the way he's treated you!

I had Evil Nikki on one shoulder and Angel Nikki on the other.

I was Contemplating my choice here for a few seconds but then evil Nikki won and I walked over to Matt, who was now in the beer section of the store.

I stood in front of him and forced him to see me, "Look, Matt, this has gone too far, I explained why I kept Sara's secret, why can't you just understand I was only trying to help?" I stated pleading with him.

"I'm not doing this here." He said being defensive and then he walked away. I went to catch up with him again, we walked side by side now.

"Well you keep ignoring me, I called you for four months, I left you a dozen messages, but you wouldn't call me back. Why won't you talk to me? Look I'm really trying here." I firmly said to him. He stopped and turned to me, his face calm but firm.

"I told you it was too late!"

He said trying to move away from me. I wasn't going to let this go so I cornered him once again and told him.

"You know you lied too, you said we would be friends forever." I hoped it made him feel guilty now.

The irritated look on his face turned into a scowl, I had used his words back on him.

"This is completely different and you know it!" He tried to whisper with anger coming from his tone by this time.

"Please Matt this has been hard for me!" I told him in my most sincere voice. I couldn't believe his behavior, why was he so angry?

He didn't say anything, just stood and crossed his tanned arms over his strong chest. He was done and now his body language was blocking me, making his stance and pretty much saying I won't listen to you anymore.

I dropped my head in defeat, It was no use, I felt drained.

Our distance in the aisle had me on one side and he on the other. I stood across from him, sad and now preparing to leave.

Just when I was ready to walk away, that cute, wonderful little kid came back around again, but this time he passed us by running full force, but not before stopping to spray Matt with a small fire extinguisher he had in his two little hands and telling him

"You need to cool off buddy!"

The youngster laughed and ran away, Matt was covered with white foam, from head to toe.

I laughed and said to him "I guess you've been educated by a kindergartener!"

With the song "Staying Alive" by the Bee Gees playing from the speaker in the store, I made sure to *strut* off to get my sandwich, with a large smile on my face I left the store in a better mood.

Chapter 8

Dim All The Lights

Last night I called Roxy and told her what happened at the grocery store. She couldn't believe the karma that came to Matt. She was laughing so much that she started snorting. Even she thought Matt was being cruel, between her laughing she said,

"Nikki, I really thought he would have come around like last month, but this is why Jessica and I took some action on your behalf."

"I know and guess what, I'm glad you guys did, he obviously is over our friendship and he hates me! Besides, I'm going out with a great guy on Saturday! He's a heart surgeon can you believe it?"

I said full of excitement!

"What no way girl, is he cute?"

"Yes, he's a catch, he's intelligent, he's so good-looking, he's another Superman, you how much I like that type.

He's athletic and he has a great career, he has his own money, he seems very independent and he surfs can you believe that, he's the whole package!"

"He does sound like a great guy, so where are you guys going on your first date?"

"Get this we are going on a hot air balloon ride to the vineyard for dinner."

"Girl, give me the details on it later." She replied with enthusiasm!

"You know it!"

For this evening's date, I decided to wear a pair of jeans and my brown leather boots, with a button-down white shirt and a yellow cashmere sweater over it.

We were instructed to wear casual clothes on the hot air balloon ride and then once we arrived at the Vineyard we would have a room to change and get ready for our dinner date.

Now for my dinner date, I decided on a strapless silk maxi dress in royal blue. I added my Carrie Bradshaw shoes (the iconic royal blue Manolo Blahnik heels) they looked stunning with my dress. I added some silver earrings and a bracelet with a matching silver necklace in a lace design and I added my white cashmere wrap for warmth. I packed everything in my garment bag and waited for the car service that was coming to pick me up.

When I arrived at Rancho Niguel Park, I saw a hot air balloon in many different colors. The balloon was beautiful, so colorful.

The driver instructed me to leave my bag in the car because he would be taking it to the vineyard for me.

"Thank you." I said.

I walked towards the team of specialists that was setting up the balloon to facilitate this fun and exciting ride.

I began chatting with one of the guys named Bruce, when Nick arrived, he came by car service as well.

"Nikki, you look wonderful." He came up and said to me

"Thank you. You look great too!"

"Ok, folks this what I need you to do."

Bruce and his buddy instructed us with a safety orientation. Plus we had a lesson on why and how the balloon doesn't have a precise landing location but there is a very large field by the vineyard and that's our target. That is basically what Bruce our facilitator said. I hope he's right!

We would also have a chaser or a car that would follow us to ensure our landing is as safe as possible.

I felt a little bit better about it now.

Next, we climbed in the basket with the pilot, Nick helped me in and then jumped in himself. He looked so cute in a pair of button-down Levi's and a navy blue wool sweater.

The late afternoon sun was hanging around turning a nice bright orange, in an hour the sun would be setting on the purple mountains. The pilot had a small picnic basket for us with champagne, we toasted to a safe balloon ride.

"Here's to making it to a second date." Nick toasted.

"Cheers." I replied.

The air was cool, and even though the sun was out it seemed to feel like a crisp Fall day.

Nick made the first move with conversation to break the ice, he asked me about the band.

"So I did some research on you and I watched a few of your performances on the internet with your band and let me just say you have an incredible voice."

"Thank you, I've been singing for about 5-6 years with the band, we do pretty well, besides Kendle's we sing at festivals, parties, and city functions, it's been fun."

"I also couldn't believe you sang with Freddie Santana." He asked with excitement.

"Yup I sure did, he's a friend of mine now, and the band Cold Creek, T-Bone, Parker, Boss, and Flick as well."

I filled Nick in on my decision not to attend law school and the path I decided to take. My family story, and my choice for moving back to Rancho Niguel and he listened with interest.

"What a story, Nikki, I admire your independence and your strength, it's nice to meet someone with some much drive."

We talked about his story, he attended Boston College and then after graduation headed out west to UCLA for medical school, he interned at UCLA Medical Center and then came out to Rancho Niguel for the last four years.

"Now you have been here in Rancho Niguel for four years why haven't I seen you around?" I asked him.

"Oh most likely it has to do with my work schedule, I have been living at Rancho General since I started working there, it literally seems that way sometimes."

Our conversation flowed naturally and we seemed in sync, with one another, we laughed at the same things, we appreciated the same charities, we both love Del La Sol Mexican Food, and we seem to have so much in common.

The burnt orange sun slowly set on the horizon, strips of dark purple filled in, and the sun hid behind the mountains.

It was like someone flipped a switch to dim all of the lights.

We saw the vineyard in the distance, the green grassy field of about five acres or maybe more lay before us, blowing in our wake.

The early evening still provided plenty of light for us to see the buildings and the gardens down below.

Our pilot directed us as best as he could and told us to hold on, we would be landing soon.

I placed my hand on the basket to brace for landing, Nick did the same, and when we slightly touched down in a mild bounce, it broke my grip and I fell into Nick who was behind me he wrapped his arms around my waist. "I got ya don't worry."

"No complaints here." I smiled and then another bounce came and we both laughed, I placed my arms over his arms and he rested his head on my shoulder.

When we safely landed, the chaser car drove up and we were escorted away to the Vineyard.

The Vineyard is a new property that came up in the last ten years, an Inn and a restaurant were added recently to the working winemaking business. We made our way to our separate rooms, my garment bag was hung and waiting for me in the closet.

I freshened up and changed into my dinner clothes.

I left my hair in light curls, my butterfly haircut gave me a nice 1977 Jacklyn Smith look.

At precisely 7 pm I went downstairs to the restaurant called Tannins. A dark wood-paneled, stately dining area with high booths in crushed velvet burgundy, dark stone flooring, and brass railings. Dim lights and soft jazz played creating a sophisticated ambiance.

"Good evening Nikki, you look amazing!"

"Thank you,"

He looked very handsome in a dark Armani suit, the cut of perfection on his athletic body. A suit that was made only for him, and polished black leather dress shoes.

Boy was he looking good!

He took my hand and we were led to our table by a host.

Our menus were already at the table, leather-bound thin books filled with culinary delights.

We had a bottle of red wine, waiting for us, and some fine sourdough bread and butter curls.

We ordered a steak for me and lamb chops for him, we drank our wine and began to discuss, our friends.

I told him about my friends in the band, Roxy my bestie, and about Jessica, Martin and Oliver, Mrs. Green, Craig, and Kiana, and Daisy and Tito.

He told me about some of the doctors he played golf with, he went on a fishing trip with Dr. Taylor Ferguson, his college fraternity bro, the one who put his name in the game.

"I'm going to have to personally thank Dr. Ferguson, for entering you into this dating service."

"It's me that should thank Roxy." He smiled at me.

When our dinner arrived we ate and talked and then laughed at some of our favorite comedians, Chapelle, Jo Koy, Chris Rock, Fluffy (Gabriel Iglesias), and many more.

"Ok we have to go to see a comedy show, I heard Fluffy is coming to town soon, maybe we can catch his show."

I told him between bites of a baked potato.

"That sounds like a plan, and maybe we can fit in some surfing."

"Now you're talking."

After dinner, we had Crème Brûlée and port and discussed having a second date.

"I think it's safe to say, we want another date, Nick."

"Absolutely, Nikki, where have you been hiding."

I smiled...

Chapter 9

Grease Lightening

We gathered our belongings from the guest rooms and Nick and I

walked to his Corvette that was parked in front of the Inn. Resting in a

circular entryway, where more fast or exotic cars were parked,

the valet drove up with the vette.

Nick opened the passenger door for me, placed our garment bags in the

front trunk, and then tipped the valet with a $50.00 dollar bill, so

generous wow.

"Thank you, sir" The valet replied to him.

Nick put his seat belt on, and then he pushed a button that slid the top

of the convertible open, and the fresh summer air gently blew in our

hair.

It was still early, only 10 pm or so, I enjoyed the ride in this beautiful

muscle machine as we cruised on.

The streets were generally empty at this hour with the exception of

some young drivers cruising the boulevard.

There must have been a rally or a meet-up for car enthusiasts because joining us on the road were: three Ford Mustangs, two Subaru STIs, three Toyota Supras, one Nissan GTR, a Subaru BRZs, and about five or six Challengers, Chargers, and another three Corvettes.

We cruised along down the road with them, the music blaring to "Rise" By Herb Albert. The other drivers gave Nick the thumbs-up sign, and some of them said "That's a dope ride dude."

One guy at the stop light asked us if we wanted to race in the mall parking lot.

"No, I'm on a date tonight, besides it's illegal, we're just cruising tonight." Nick waved him off.

"Ok, man, but it's blocked off, the police do that so we can race and not hurt anyone, it opens after 10 pm, the entry charge is $20 bucks and it goes to charity. It's legit and put on by the city and some community of moms." The driver told us from his open car window.

Nick looked at me "What do you think?"

I was feeling adventurous so I said "Ok!"

"We'll be there!" Nick told the driver.

We drove to the mall parking lot on the east side where the lot was as large as the Disneyland parking lot, ok one of their sections of the lot. We paid the $20 bucks and drove in through the entrance of orange cones that led to the racing area. It was just like the kid said, the race strip was blocked off with two lanes and a metal gate that the onlookers stood behind. The banner at the front entrance read MOMS FOR SAFE RACING.

There were parents, teenagers, adults, a private ambulance and a private security company, and a small snack truck.

We drove to the starting point, where we had to wait our turn to race. Two cars were before us, a Shelby Mustang and a Chevy Camaro.

"Nikki, do you want to sit in the stands or do you want to ride with me?"

"I'd like to stay if that's all right."

He smiled "Now you'll be able to see what this car can do."

I returned my smile and told him,

"Let's win!"

Our turn came up and we drove to the starting lane next to the car competing against us, a white Porsche 911 GT3 to be exact!

I tightened my seat belt, Nick had his hand on the steering wheel ready to use the paddle shifters.

Ok so Corvette hear me out, why oh why did they take this beautiful vehicle and put paddle shifters on it? A real car enthusiast wants a stick shift and a clutch, the paddle shifters are so kindergarten, I mean really it's a wonder we don't have a hole in the floor to use foot power to make it go. Without a stick shift, it takes all of the fun out of it, real manual transmissions have a stick shift and a clutch, maybe next year

Chevy will get it right. Just my opinion. I know shut up Nikki!

The flag went down and Nick charged ahead, I held on to the sides of

my seat as I felt this car speed down the lane. We were running neck

and neck, we sped up then the Porsche sped up. Nick shifted his baby

paddles again and then he said "Watch this."

He hit the gas and then we took off!

The car sped past the Porsche by a lot and we won! Nick slowed down

and then we finally came to a stop at the end of the parking lot where

concrete barricades stood.

He made a U-turn and then drove to the winner's lot, he parked the car

and we got out and laughed and jumped up and down!

It was so much fun the rush of adrenalin and the speed, the intensity,

the thrill of the race, it was like gliding across the road, I can't even

describe it anymore.

I hugged Nick and he picked me up and spun me around!

"Was that amazing, didn't I say trust me?" He was all smiles and we

were like two teenagers, giddy and excited.

"Nikki!" I heard my name and turned around to see Sara and Jagger

coming toward us.

"Nikki you were awesome you guys won!" She hugged me. You look gorgeous, Oh my God you're on a date, oh I'm so sorry, I didn't mean to interrupt.

"No it's fine, meet Dr. Nick Williams, Nick this is Sara, she's my friend and my employee." I smiled brightly.

"Nice to meet you, Sara." Nick shook her hand, he was still happy from the endorphins charging in his body.

"Hi It's nice to meet you, this is my boyfriend Jagger."

"Hey dude your car is way cool, can I take a look!" Jagger responded like a little kid in a candy store.

"Sure come on." Nick was showing Jagger his car they were talking about the engine and the brakes.

Sara leaned in and gave me her opinion on Nick.

"Nikki, he's really cute, did you guys just meet?"

"Roxy set me up on Linked to Your Heart the matchmaking service and I went to this speed dating event and I met Nick and we have been hitting it off. This is our first date, we went on a hot air balloon ride and then we just came back from dinner at the Vineyard and then we decided to come to this race.

Oh my gosh, I still can't believe we did that, oh Sara, it's been a long time since I had so much fun!" I said grabbing Sara's hands and shaking.

"I can see that Nikki, you look so happy." She chuckled.

"I am, I'm having fun!" I let go of her by now and rubbed my arms from excitement, and a little bit of a chill my cashmere wrap was in the passenger seat.

Nick and Jagger came back over to us.

"Miss Nikki, I have to get Sara back before her curfew but it was nice to see you again."

"Yeah, I gotta go or my brother will be mad and then I'll get an hour-long phone call from my parents."

"Ok drive safe guys." I hugged Sara again and they waved bye.

I turned to Nick and told him,

"Thank you, Nick, I haven't had this much fun in a long time."

"Same here, it's nice to take a break from the hospital."

We got back in the car and made our way back to my place, we were stopped at a red light, and we were smiling and talking about how he pulled ahead of the Porsche and how cool it was. When the light turned green Nick gunned it a bit too much, we were still coming down from our rush, we were still feeling the excitement when all of a sudden a black Charger with blue and red flashing lights (berries and cherries) drove behind us. Nick pulled over to the side of the road and took out his license and his proof of insurance.

"Oh no, I guess I gunned it a little too much."

Nick made a silly face.

I laughed!

"Oh no, you might get a ticket." I laughed again.

On Nick's driver's side, Paul walked up to the car and Detective Sonya came up to my side. "Nikki is that you?"

I looked at Sonya and then at Paul, I wanted to disappear at this moment.

"It's a lovely evening tonight isn't it." I said.

Sonya smiled, girlfriend knew it was an awkward moment for me.

Paul gave Nick a once over.

Then he looked over at me.

"Yeah, Nikki introduce us."

His green eyes were icy!

"I'm on a date, this is Doctor Nick Williams III, he's a cardiac surgeon at Rancho General and this is his amazing car." I did the Vanna White impression showcasing the beautiful leather dashboard with my hands. I smiled at him, but Paul had no reaction.

"Hello, I'm Detective Sonya Smith a friend of Nikki's."

Sonya interjected to break the awkwardness of this scene.

"Nice to meet you." Nick smiled then he turned to Paul.

"I'm sorry officer, we just won a race over at the mall and I guess I was still a little high on our win." He was trying to explain.

"A Corvette Z06, yeah they go about 200 mph, that's pretty fast!" Paul replied.

"I told Nick, I haven't had this much fun in a long time, and he was so gracious to indulge me."

Sonya didn't want to look amused so she looked in the other direction.

Paul didn't say anything more except,

"I'm going to give you a warning today Doctor, slow it down grease lightning!" Paul handed Nick his license and gave me a strange look!

"Thank you." He replied taking his license back.

When they walked back to the cruiser Nick laughed it off, and asked me "What was that about?"

"That was my ex-boyfriend..."

Chapter 10

Rumors

Last night after Nick dropped me off, we stood by the door, saying good night. "I think this was by far the best date ever." I told him.

"I have to agree Nikki, I don't think I've ever had this much excitement in one day and I perform heart surgery."

We laughed it off but then he looked into my eyes and put his arm around my waist, we edged closer to one another and we kissed.

After our kiss, I said good night and closed the door. I felt like shouting at the top of the roof "Yes!!!"

Nikki is back to her old self, with no more heartbreak...

Roxy called me this morning around 9 am, it seemed like the gossip wheel was already turning, she said she found out from Jessica this morning while getting her venti Americano that when Paul came in an hour before to get his grande hazelnut latte, he asked her if she knew a Doctor Nick Williams. Apparently, he told Jessica that he is the new guy Nikki is dating, he called him some hot shot surgeon that drives a nice Corvette."

Jessica said she told Paul that Nikki met him at LINKED TO THE HEART.

My other line on the phone started beeping, it was Jessica.

"Hey Roxy hold on a sec it's Jessica."

"Ok!"

"Hi Jess, I'm on the other line with Roxy."

"She beat me, I was going to call sooner but we got slammed this morning."

"Don't worry, she filled me in on what Paul said."

"Oh, but she didn't hear what Matt said when he came in a few minutes ago."

"Oh no way, did I tell you what happened to Matt at Sprouts?"

"Yeah, I heard from Roxy, but get this he comes in today and like casually says to me *so Sara said she saw Nikki last night and Nikki was with some rich doctor in a Corvette Z06 and they won some car race at the mall.*"

"Oh, no way!" I replied.

"Yes, way! And if that wasn't enough he goes like this he says *So have you met this guy?* I was ready to start busting out to say hey dude you missed your opportunity with Nikki and now that some incredible guy is dating her now you are concerned. Guys I don't get them. Oh, I gotta go I have customers see ya I'll talk later."

She hung up and I went back to my conversation with Roxy

"Listen to this Roxy."

After my call with Roxy, I decided to call Martin and Oliver and see if they wanted to get breakfast at Pastries of Paris in the mall.

"Nikki I was just thinking about you." Oliver said answering the phone on the first ring.

"Are you guys available to go to breakfast?"

"You have gossip." I heard him snap his finger and he replied

"We'll meet you there in fifteen minutes."

We sat outside on the patio of the cafe, I ordered my favorite the French toast with bacon and fresh fruit.

"Ok Nikki, so tell us what's new?" Martin asked taking a sip of his coffee.

I gave them the rundown on the evidence I found at Kristin's place, the flash drive videos, and that Craig was more than grateful to have the evidence. Who knows maybe they can find a way to clear up the video.

"So Nikki, do they have a suspect?" Oliver asked.

"Not that I've heard, when Mrs. Green and I had a meeting with Paul it seemed like they had nothing!"

I said as I took a bite of my bacon.

"Here's what I'm wondering It's obvious that the killer is someone she is close with, a co-worker, a boyfriend, so then why not interview all of the staff, there is bound to be some gossip that might lead to a clue." Martin suggested.

"I agree Martin, you know what I can ask Mrs. Green to do a run down for me. She might have the best insight."

"You're right Nikki, but then why not ask your new friend, Nick, he might know some of the chatter that goes on at the nurse's station too!" Oliver suggested.

"Oh no, who told you guys about my date?"

"Roxy called us last night, we were just hoping you could fill in the gaps." Martin smiled.

"We had a hell of a time, I was so high on life! It was fun, I felt like a teenager again."

I told them about our car race and seeing Sara and Jagger and then to end the excitement of the night the run-in with Paul and Sonya.

Oliver was holding his stomach laughing.

"Oh Nikki, no more! I can just picture the look on Nick's face when you told him that was my ex. Oh that's crazy, what were the odds?"

"Guys according to Roxy via Jessica this morning Paul had said he and Sonya were checking out a lead on the murder case when they saw this sports car hall ass down the street. He told Sonya right when he hit the lights It's probably some guy trying to impress a hot chick."

We all laughed!

"Little did he know." Martin added.

"You should have seen Sonya's face she had to look away to keep from cracking up.

I felt bad for Nick, he had no idea who these people were and what was going on here." I managed to say between sips of my coffee.

We were having a good time, but the guys gave me a good idea about the case, I had to talk to Mrs. Green.

"So I have an idea I'm going to call Mrs. Green and we can have a meeting and see if we can find out more about Kristin and her co-workers, let's meet tomorrow night at my place I'll make some seafood and sausage cajun packets for dinner."

"We'll bring the wine." Oliver volunteered.

"I'll have Roxy and Jessica bring dessert."

"Sounds like a plan." Martin said.

We were wrapping up breakfast when Martin called out.

"Hey Matt."

I looked over at Martin and shook my head no, but I heard footsteps coming up behind me.

Oliver looked confused he mouthed silently "What happened?"

I just frowned and he looked worried.

"Hi, Guys, and Nikki." He said sounding disappointed he had to see me.

I looked up at him but he was looking away still trying to avoid me. I managed a "Hi."

"Why don't you join us Matt?" Martin asked still clueless.

"No, I'm just picking up an order to go, I have to get to work."

I sat there silent not knowing how to approach him, I still had this Vision of him covered in white foam, and the image of that little boy saying cool off buddy.

I wanted to laugh but I kept a straight face. Why was I enjoying this so much? Bad Nikki was resting on my shoulder again.

"Maybe next time Matt, say come by the gallery I have a new sculpture that we just got in I know you'll love it."

"Thanks." He went in to get his food and when he was out of sight, I chuckled.

"Ok, spill it Nikki tell me everything?" Oliver begged!

In the short three minutes before Matt came back out I told Martin and Oliver about the Sprouts incident.

"Oh no Nikki, no wonder he didn't want to speak to you." Oliver chimed.

"Oh, you two have the funniest foreplay." Martin said smiling.

"Are you kidding he *hates* me?" I told them with gusto!

"Nikki, he doesn't hate you, he's furious with you but he doesn't hate you, that's impossible!" Martin stated.

"Oh, Martin I think you just adore us too much!" I said with a pout.

Matt came walking out of the restaurant with a bag in his hand. He waved at Martin and Oliver and just looked at me and said "Humph!"(that sound one makes when they have displeasure or contempt for someone or something), yes I know that sound well.

Chapter 11

"Kiss My Grits"

I flipped the channel several times until I settled on a vintage TV channel called Kid Retro.

An episode of Alice was on, the 1970s -1980s show with the lead character Alice (Linda Lavin) who worked as a waitress in a small diner for Mel her overly loud, and angry, but teddy bear of a boss/owner, then there was the timid and silly co-worker Vera. The funny and sassy pants co-worker Flo, she always yelled out one of my favorite lines, "Kiss My Grits" I remember always laughing hysterically when she said that.

I love these old shows they were so much fun!

 I finished watching TV and then I called Mrs. Green and told her about our plan for a group brainstorming session to come up with some ideas about solving Kristin's murder.

She thought it was a good idea and she asked if we could help her with funeral arrangements for Kristin. She needed florals, and a selection of food, she already had a guest list and she needed some dedication ideas.

Mrs. Green had already spoken to Father Riley at St. Mark's Catholic Church, our parish. The burial was going to be at Forest Hills cemetery. The reception was going to be held in the garden room at the Cafe Gothic and Inn. The funeral would be held next week, the day after the grand re-opening of Kendle's, boy was my calendar looking busy these days. I sent text messages to Jessica, Roxy, Martin and Oliver, and Tito and Daisy.

I figured it would be best to have a larger pool of ideas and bodies in motion.

This afternoon I went off to get some seafood and other items for my foil packets, for this evening's meeting. I didn't want to go to Sprouts at the risk of running into Matt again so I opted for Vons.

I selected some nice wild shrimp from Mexico, and some scallops fresh from the East Coast.

I managed to find some fresh herbs rosemary, thyme, and some organic flat-leaf parsley. Two lemons and four ears of corn, some red potatoes, and a large yellow onion.

I went off to search for the andouille sausage, going down the aisle I found what I was looking for and grabbed up three packages of them. It looked as though I had everything, except beverages, Martin and Oliver were bringing wine but I also like having a variety so I thought of getting some other selections in the soda aisle and beer aisle. I placed some Coke, Ginger Ale, and some Root Beer in my basket along with some iced tea and Waterloo-flavored sparkling water. I headed over to the refrigerated beer aisle next.

This aisle was a little busy, after all, it was Saturday. I selected a nice IPA and then searched for the Blue Moon down the way that had become a favorite for Martin and me.

Should I get the six-pack or the larger pack hmm?

"Strange I've never seen you here before."

Oh crap, I silently kicked myself, I forgot this store is right across from Paul's apartment complex.

I wanted to leave right now because this wasn't happening, What were the odds?

He looked very casual in a black baseball cap, Levis, and a black t-shirt, those awesome muscled arms of his stretched the t-shirt he wore.

I played it cool, and just did what I do best under pressure I lied!

"Everyone knows how good the seafood here is."

"It looks like you have enough for an army." He said placing a pack of Modelo, Pacifico, and Coors in his basket.

"Just a few friends coming over. What about you? That's a lot of beer!"

"Poker game tonight, a rematch, Craig wants to win his money back from the chief." He smiled with satisfaction.

This was a breakthrough he wasn't cold with me, more like his old self, as if he wanted to talk to me again.

"I would pay to see that." I chuckled since Craig was always the one getting money from everyone else.

He laughed too "I bet you would."

Since he was in a good mood, I figured Nikki just go for it and ask about the investigation, hopefully, he wouldn't bolt.

"Anything new in the investigation." I asked casually.

"Nothing I can share with you." The temperature dropped a few degrees in his tone.

So I shot back, cool and calm but with sarcasm in my tone.

"So what else is new?" I turned my shopping cart to leave the aisle but Paul followed and responded with...

"We have some possible suspects." Both of our carts stood side by side.

"Who are you guys looking at." I asked with curiosity, this was the first big break I had heard of in the case besides the flash drive.

I also figured I could ask him if it came from the video, Did they get the tech department to fix the quality of the video?

Did they have a face of the doctor in the video snorting coke? I had so many questions for him.

He was just about to give me an answer when I heard another familiar voice coming toward us.

"Oh Paul, I knew I'd find you here!" She was dressed in her black Yoga pants showing way too much baby got back. Paired with a cropped white T-shirt and her fancy Nike athletic shoes, and a Louie Vuitton bag slung over her shoulder.

Stacie sashayed over to us and flung her hair in my direction as she made her way between Paul and me and completely ignoring the fact that I was there.

I didn't want to stick around and watch this so

I moved up ahead with my basket, heading out of the aisle.

I heard Paul tell her "Give me just one minute."

He walked to catch up to me and then said,

"Thank you for the flash drive Nikki." He wanted to say more but then he stopped, and I broke the awkwardness.

"You're welcome, I hope you guys have a nice evening."

He smiled and then walked back over to his basket and Stacie.

I could barely hear her say,

"We have time to get dinner before your poker game."

I went to the nearest cashier to go check out. I whispered to myself

Oh, kiss my grits, Stacie!

Chapter 12

Dinner And A Mystery

I had the foil packets on the grill outside on my patio, I had put potatoes, small cobbs of corn, sliced andouille sausage, onion, carrots, and herbs and I closed them in foil and cooked them until the potatoes were almost tender, I added the seasoned shrimp and grilled the packets on low for a few minutes and then removed them.

Next, I made bacon-wrapped scallops and popped them in the oven at 350 for 15-20 minutes. I made an orange dipping sauce from marmalade, soy sauce, fresh lime juice, scallions, and salt to taste, to go with them, and set the appetizers out on a plate. My guests arrived and now we were at the table enjoying a scrumptious dinner.

"These are so good," Daisy remarked as she started on her second packet.

Martin poured more wine around the table, filling everyone's glass.

"I just want to say thank you to our host for this evening, Nikki, you can cook for us anytime."

"Thank you, Martin, you guys are great." I held up my glass and toasted "To friendship."

"Here, here!" Everyone responded.

Mrs. Green thanked everyone next.

"I just want to thank everyone for coming to help me, this has been very difficult for me and I really appreciate all of you for your help on this case." Her eyes were red and watery now.

"We're always here for you Mrs. Green." Tito replied.

"I second that!" Roxy echoed the sentiment.

We raised our glasses again!

After we finished our meal, Jessica served up some apple pie and coffee, Roxy, and Daisy did the dishes for me and Martin, Oliver, and Tito, cleaned the grill, and took out the trash. When we all settled in the living room I took out a notebook.

"Ok let's start with the funeral, Mrs. Green, I called the florist and we have two arrangements at the reception, a spray over the casket and two wreaths in the church, all in white and pink flowers. You mentioned peonies were her favorite right?"

"Perfect Nikki." Mrs. Green said.

"I can call Cafe Gothic and talk to the event planner there, I know her and she can probably give you a good price, on the food for the event." Roxy added.

"Thank you, my budget has room for some extras, Kristin's parents left her a substantial amount of money so I'm ok with the cost."

We went over a few other items, times, dates, pallbearers, and speeches that some of her co-workers wanted to be a part of. We wrapped it up on that end and moved to the investigation.

"I have some news, it's first hand and the source is on the case." I began.

"Craig actually shared something new." Martin asked.

"Um, no it was from another person." I trailed off.

"You spoke with Paul didn't you?" Oliver asked.

I was taken aback a little, I didn't know what to say at this point but they were all looking at me for the answer.

"Yes, ok I did, I ran into him at Vons, and I forgot he lives across the street. Anyway, I asked him if there was anything new on the case and he said they have three possible suspects that they are looking at."

"Did he say anything else?" Daisy asked curiously.

I made a face "No, Stacie came by and interrupted our conversation."

"What!" "On No!" "Come on!" These were the many responses from all over the room from my group of friends here.

"Oh yeah! If that wasn't bad enough she flung her hair in my face when she wedged in between Paul and me."

"How dare she." Jessica said annoyed.

"After that I left, I went to pay for my groceries but I think Paul is on to something especially because I gave Craig a clue, a big one. Mrs. Green remember the flash drive we found at Kristin's?"

"Yes." She replied.

"Well I was able to look at it with Craig and it had two videos, one of Kristin explaining she had been threatened by a fellow doctor because she saw him snorting coke right before he was going into surgery."

"Oh no!" Mrs. Green covered her mouth with her hand in complete shock!

"So it's someone at the hospital, oh my, I was afraid of that." She choked out, feeling disappointed.

Everyone else was catching up on the story, except for Martin and Oliver who already knew. The others, all looked slapped by the new evidence I brought forward.

"We do know one thing the suspect is male." Roxy said.

"I don't know if that narrows it down, guys." I replied.

"It's a start Nikki, I need to go back and spend some time at the hospital." Mrs. Green offered.

A simple plan that was working its way into her mind.

"Everyone else keep your ears open." I suggested.

Chapter 13

The Love Boat

Linked to Your Heart contacted me, and gave me the information for the follow-up podcast. The day had come and I had to be at the LINKED TO THE HEART headquarters in Los Angeles by 3 pm today, I was asked to dress casually.

I opted for a pair of jeans, with a sleeveless turquoise top and some white vans. Nick called me and asked if he could pick me up and we would drive together to the studio.

"Sure, that sounds good."

"Ok, I'll pick you up at 1:30 pm."

After heavy traffic, we made it there ten minutes early and instantly we were pulled in many directions to get ready for the live podcast.

We sat next to one another on a small sofa, a coffee table in front of us held three mics that had been set up. Two leather chairs joined us with CeeCee and her assistant.

"Ok ya'll we go live in 3 2 1"

We were live now and she began her live podcast with her larger-than-life personality.

"CeeCee Sass here today with my company LINKED TO THE HEART, we are sponsored by Love's BBQ sauce, a sweet and tangy and full of spices sauce you can slather on your ribs or use it over grilled chicken, or just enjoy as a dipping sauce, remember Link Love's BBQ sauce to your heart." She wrapped up her spiel and then began the discussion with Nick and me.

"So today I have here the beautiful Nikki Rodriguez and the handsome Nick Williams III. Now you two went on a fabulous date, we had our camera crew there secretly filming a few of your moments from beginning to end. Let's roll a bit of it."

Up on a screen to our right was a collage of our date, a scene from when we took off in the hot air balloon to the scene where I fell into Nick's arms and then on our date when we entered the restaurant, the toast of champagne we had and the view of us driving off in Nicks Corvette.

After the reel ended CeeCee brought her attention back to Nick

"So, tell me darlin' did you make a connection with Nikki?"

"I sure did. Nikki is a fun and kind person, we had an amazing time. At the end of the evening, we even raced my car at the mall, a MOMs

87

FOR SAFE RACING event, and we had a blast! " Nick said answering CeeCee's question.

"How about you, honey?" She asked me.

"Yes, I did. The race was awesome and we won, so we were very excited about that! Nick is a great driver." He smiled at me.

"I saw that beautiful blue Corvette of yours Nick, how fast does it go?" She asked in a flirty way.

"I think we hit 200mph," he told her but looked at me for confirmation.

"Yeah I think so, it was fast." I responded in agreement.

"I also heard ya'll were stopped by the police on the way home?" Nick chuckled but reluctantly told CeeCee.

"Yes, I was still excited from my win and when my red light turned green I hit the gas a bit too hard"

Nick confessed.

"I heard ya'll were pulled over by Nikki's ex-boyfriend Detective Paul Anderson." She said reading this information off of an index card she had with her.

We both looked blindsided by this part of the conversation. I had to defuse this bomb and fast, this wasn't a tabloid magazine here.

"Yes CeeCee, that's true but everything was fine." I smiled.

"Oh, honey that's what we call an awkward moment." She laughed a large and noisy laugh.

Nick and I sat silently not knowing what to say next, we didn't want this to turn into a gossip party.

"All right let's hear what the listeners have to say. Vote for where we are going to send these two on their next date.

Will it be the Disneyland day trip, the Natural History Museum adventure, or the Queen Marie IV cruiser for brunch?

Get your votes in now!"

CeeCee checked her laptop computer that her assistant brought over to her. After chatting for a few minutes about how cool the hot air balloon ride was, CeeCee gathered the results of the vote.

"I'm getting the results now and well boys and girls it looks like Nick and Nikki will be going on a cruise brunch on the Queen Marie IV, does that sound like fun."

She shouted out.

Nick and I nodded "That sounds wonderful." I replied.

"Ok listeners tune in next week when we bring Nick and Nikki back from their brunch on The Love Boat in Long Beach, remember we'll have our cameras there as well."

We signed off, and CeeCee got up from her chair and gave me a barely-there hug, but with Nick, she wrapped her arms around him for a tight hug. "Gimme some sugar baby!"

Nick looked uncomfortable with her, but then she broke away, straightened her shirt, and cupped her boobs!

"I still got it, baby." She laughed out loud with her assistant smiling and agreeing with her. "I'll be in my dressing room, ya'll bye"

Then she walked off!

Chapter 14

Welcome Back Kendle's

July 1st arrived faster than I thought it would, the grand opening was set for today and I had about a million things to do.

I invited Nick to the event this afternoon at around 4 pm. He said he had four-hour surgery starting at 9 am but that he would try to make it.

When I arrived at Kendle's the kitchen staff was running around prepping food, and my servers were placing crystal salt and pepper shakers on the tables, the new hostesses were making sure all reservations were in order. Everyone was moving and working.

Sara was at the front desk, she had her training in the last two weeks and was beyond excited to be working here.

"Good morning boss, everything at the front desk is ready." Sara loved her new uniform too! We went with light blue a-line fit and flair dresses with a comfort pump in nude, for the hostesses. My servers all wore khaki-colored pants, with a long sleeve light blue button-down linen dress shirt, no tie, and brown shoes. I got the idea from a summer clothing catalog, I presented it to my servers and they loved it.

"Great job Sara, let's go outside for the ribbon cutting."

I led my staff outside of the new and improved Kendle's Restaurant. The mayor and Stacie had just arrived in the black Lincoln limo, and a large crowd of the community stood waiting patiently for us to open our doors. Many were taking photos of the new building or selfies with the restaurant behind them.

"It looks wonderful! Mayor CJ blared out.

Again Stacie rolled her eyes behind the mayor's back, she was already done with her today.

I saw a lot of my friends waiting patiently, Martin, Oliver, Jessica, and Mrs. Green, they waved to me.

My staff, Chef Stark, Roxy, Tito, and Daisy stood next to me. The mayor handed me the makeshift scissors and she introduced me.

"Welcome everyone, I'd like to thank you all for coming to support the grand re-opening of the new Kendle's restaurant, and now our very own owner and operator Nikki Rodriguez."

Cheers, and clapping from the audience came for me.

"Thank you for being here everyone."

I cut the ribbon and light blue and white balloons were released. There were cheers, and clapping all around the crowd here.

We opened the doors and now it was time to get down to business.

The mayor took my hand as I walked in the front double doors, "Nikki thank you for reserving a special table for Stacie and me and did I mention we added three more guests."

"Yes, it's all taken care of Ms. Mayor, not to worry!"

I led Mayor CJ and Stacie upstairs to our new terrace that faced the mountain views, with a small fountain off to the side.

The umbrellas were open providing shade, and my servers were pleasantly waiting to serve customers.

I sat them down at one of our finest tables and right away my server brought glasses of filtered ice water.

"Enjoy your dinner." I smiled and went back downstairs to seat more customers.

After seating two more couples I walked back to the front desk, the next customer coming in from the double doors was Paul.

Before he could reach the desk I told Sara, "I'll be right back I'm going to check on something."

I turned to leave but Paul called me out "Nikki, can I speak with you for just a moment."

He was dressed in a nice white dress shirt, and navy blue pants, his Oakley glasses on his head, and his bright greenish blue eyes dashing as always.

It was useless to think of him this way anymore because we had already gone our own ways but having him around all the time made it harder.

"Sure." I replied.

"Paul it's nice to see you again." Sara called out.

"Sara, wow you're working here now, that's great."

"Yeah, thanks to Nikki." She smiled.

"I'll catch up later Sara." Paul waved.

We walked away from the desk "So what's going on?" I asked him.

"I just wanted you to know, that we have to interview every doctor that worked with Kristin, and one of the 20 surgeons we will be interviewing is Nick."

"Oh! Well you don't have anything to worry about, he's not involved in any of this."

Paul looked at me sympathetically he replied "Yeah you're right, you've always been a good judge of character Nikki."

Why was he telling me this? To warn me or to get a rise out of me.

"I have to get back to work, I go on stage in twenty minutes, If you want to stay I can find you a table."

"I uh, actually I'm meeting Stacie and the Mayor here." He said in a soft tone.

"Oh, sure, I'll take you to their table." I walked Paul upstairs, he was impressed with the place.

"Oh Nikki, you did an amazing job here, this place is beautiful." He complimented me.

"Thanks, here you are." I said leading him outside on the patio to join his party.

"Paul, I'm so glad you're here." Stacie stood up and practically pulled Paul over to a chair beside her." I just raised my eyebrows and walked away.

An hour later I was busy taking questions from customers, they gave me compliments on the new place and some customers wanted photos with me. Tito was working the upstairs bar, he had a glass of iced water waiting for me on the counter.

"Don't forget to hydrate boss."

"Thank you, Tito." I chugged it down.

"Nikki, we go on in fifteen minutes." Roxy came by reminding me.

"Thanks!"

I stopped by the office to quickly change into my little black dress and stilettos and I fixed my makeup.

I walked downstairs and joined my band, We started playing some soft tunes since it was early, So I opened with "The Closer I Get To You" By Roberta Flack and the late great Donnie Hathaway.

Since the lovely song is a duet I had Tito come down and sing with me.
He has been begging me for months now and when he auditioned for
me we were all blown away. We had no idea he could sing so well.
The downstairs bar was crowded with customers listening to our music,
and some were on the small dance floor. Paul had come down from
upstairs and had a glass of ginger ale in his hand, Nick stood by the
entrance, I smiled at him and he winked at me.

Tito and I sang next to one another, the duet came out so perfectly.
Everyone clapped when the song was over: "Let's give a big hand for
Tito in his first appearance with Little Black Dress." He had whistles
and cheers, and Daisy blushed and blew him a kiss.

"Thank you, everyone, thank you." He was all smiles now.

We started another song, "I Just Wanna Stop" By Gino Vannelli.

I saw Mrs. Green sitting with a man in his 30s or 40s a good-looking
Italian man, and I wondered if he was Kristin's, Mr. Giacomo.

Mayor CJ and Stacie were coming downstairs, the mayor stood off
watching us play, she noticed Mr. Giacomo and went to say hi to him. It
seemed they knew each other well.

Stacie sauntered to Paul who was still working on his ginger ale,
slowly, and even though she tugged at him he stood still just watching
the band.

Nick sat on a bar stool drinking a beer, he enjoyed our music and smiled at me each time I looked his way. Cute flirting I call it!

We decided to take our dinner break and I told everyone we would be back in 45 minutes, I walked toward the bar to Nick, and he greeted me with a glass of ice water, "The bartender Ken said you needed this."

"Thank you." I took a long drink.

Stacie only two seats away tugged at Paul again and whispered something in his ear, he put his drink down and smiled at her, then he looked at me, with a lingering look before he walked out with her.

I didn't understand what was going on with him, the last four months he was as cold as ice and now he's speaking to me again like we've been friends forever. I don't understand.

"You sound amazing up there."

Nick said complimenting me.

"Thank you." I replied and we were making conversation about Tito's singing when Mrs. Green tapped me on the shoulder,

"Nikki I hate to interrupt but I'd like you to meet someone."

"Hi, Mrs. Green." Nick said.

"Hi, Dr. Williams, it's nice to see you again." She smiled.

Just then the gentleman that was sitting with Mrs. Green introduced himself.

"I'm Donnie Giacomo, I was a very good friend of Kristin's, it's nice to meet you." he shook my hand.

Nick set his beer down.

"Nikki I have to get going, I'll see you on our next date. You were great up there."

"Oh ok, sure I'll see you on our date." Nick said bye to Mrs. Green and Mr. Giacomo and left pretty fast.

I figured maybe he has an early morning, I looked at my watch it was only 7:15 pm and the sun wasn't even set yet.

We went back to the booth Mrs. Green and Donnie were sitting at, we sat down and Mrs. Green immediately said "Nikki, Donnie, and I have been talking and he wants to be a part of our investigation team." Chef Stark showed up at our table next, he and Donnie obviously knew each other already "Donnie, my buddy, how are you doing?"

"I've been better." He commented.

"Nikki, I told Donnie about your excellent sleuthing skills and that I believe you can help find clues to solving this horrific crime." Chef Stark told me.

Donnie spoke up "If it's the last thing I do, I will get justice for my Kristin, her killer will be found."

"I'll do everything I can to help." I assured him.

"Thank you, Tony speaks very highly of you, so if he trusts you I trust you." He pointed to himself.

"I need to get back to the kitchen, Donnie I'll call you tomorrow we'll have lunch."

"Thank you, Tony, We'll talk tomorrow." They shook hands and Chef Tony Stark went back to the kitchen.

"Mr. Giacomo, do you have any idea who would do this to her?"

"Like I told the police Kristin said she had a problem with a co-worker, a doctor, she never gave me a name but she said he was someone she knew very well. She just said they had a conflict over an issue!"

"This is going to be difficult."

Chapter 15

Macho Man

I slept in today because we were so busy last night, Kendle's finally closed at 11:30 pm, and all of the staff left at midnight.

The overwhelming response was positive, Kendle's was a huge success! Today Daisy and Tito were closing and Roxy was taking my 11 am shift. I had a boat to catch.

Brunch was at 11:30 am today, the second date that Nick and I would have. I chose a nice summer dress, a white eyelet maxi dress with a white belt and a slit off the side. I added a sun straw wide-brim hat with a white band around it, an ode to the 1970s model in a Cosmopolitan magazine.

Nick picked me up right on time.

"Hi, you look beautiful."

"Hello and Thank you." I said sliding into the soft leather seats.

The car growled onto the freeway, and we drove the toll lane to bypass all of the traffic.

"So you missed a great show at the end of the evening, we didn't close until 11:30 pm."

"Yeah, I'm sorry about that I was so tired from that surgery it was a big one." He trailed off.

We discussed some of his work, he told me about some of the surgeries he has had and I told him about my own health scare back in February when my heart stopped.

"I remember hearing about that, one of the doctors in my area consulted with Dr. Hudson your doctor, and well you know doctors talk in the lounge. I never knew you were the patient, what a small world."

Just then I got a text from Martin.

Hi Nikki,

I have a small favor to ask

Oliver and I were asked by Matt

to help him plan Sara's sweet 16th birthday party it's a disco theme.

(Yes Oliver had a hand in the theme! Ha ha)

She is set on having it in the new banquet room at Kendle's

Her parents are paying for it and they gave Matt a budget to stick to.

It's actually pretty generous, she's allowed to have about 80-100 guests

and a band, food, cake the works. It's in two weeks

because her birthday falls on a Saturday this year, so what do you

say?"

I replied to Martin.

"It's fine by me, we don't have any parties in there yet so tell her

to send out her invites. It's nice of you two to help Sara,

I know Matt wouldn't have a clue what to do."

Martin responded with:

"Thank you, Nikki, Sara is jumping up and down she's so happy!"

I put a thumbs-up emoji.

"Good News?" Nick asked.

"Yeah, Sara's 16th birthday party in two weeks at Kendle's."

"Oh boy, a room with teenagers wow!" Nick laughed.

"Sara is going with a disco theme." I laughed, thinking of Oliver and

Martin and the promised disco Wednesday we decided on a few months

ago.

We arrived in Long Beach and parked in the garage parking structure,

we walked to the QM(Queen Marie IV) a large ship that resembles an

old steam liner but is updated and sails around for two hours and serves

Sunday brunch and dinner.

We were seated pretty fast, at a nice table with a large window and a

view of the marina.

"The brunch here is a buffet so go right ahead and help yourselves."

The server told us "We have orange and peach mimosas, juices, and coffees, or if you would prefer a cocktail I can get that for you right now." She offered.

"I'll take an Old Fashioned!" Nick replied.

"I'll stick with the peach mimosa."

We walked up to the buffet, there were so many choices, a carving station with beef, and ham. A large table filled with fruits and cheeses, nuts, jams, and spreads.

The first station on the right had fresh waffles made to order, another had an omelet and or scramble station.

The large Trident ice sculpture indicated the next table was filled with seafood, a tray of ice under the platters, and stenos for the chaffing dishes.

The many selections were hot and cold: shrimp cocktail, fresh oysters, muscles, clams, crab cakes, lobster tails, wild king salmon, a seafood pasta dish, and a seafood salad.

The dessert table was filled with chocolate cakes, pies of several flavors, jello cups with whip cream, cheesecakes, lemon bars, caramel cakes, coconut cakes, and some custards and mouses.

I had never seen such a large buffet! I had a moment of not knowing what direction to turn to first.

"A little overwhelming isn't it?" Nick asked.

"Yeah, I'm not sure where to go first, there's so much great stuff!"

I ended up with some fruit, cheese, a slice of ham, and a small cheese soufflé, for my first plate. Of course, I'm going back for more stuff!

"This is round one."

Nick placed his plate down he opted for the prime rib, seafood salad, and crab cakes to start with.

"Wow, for a heart surgeon, you surprise me."

He chuckled

"I know it looks very unhealthy but it's ok to eat like this on special occasions, I eat healthy, I work out and meals like this are pretty rare, so when I have a special occasion I like to indulge, by the way, I'll be going for a slice of chocolate cake too."

He smiled.

"I'm so glad you feel that way because I'm kinda like a big foodie myself. I know to watch the cholesterol and the salt intake and I do, I work out and eat right most of the time but it's awesome to indulge here and there."

"I know the general consensus is that all doctors are healthy, and look down on this kind of food but the reality is it's not as bad as people think. All in moderation right?"

"I agree."

We chatted over the beautiful view, now that we were sailing on the water now!

"So, I'm helping Mrs.Green with the funeral, it's this week and I was wondering are you coming?"

"Yes, I won't be able to stay for very long but I'll be there, and so will a bunch of us from the hospital that knew Kristin."

"How well did you know her, I mean did she assist in the OR?"

"I believe she became a CVOR (cardiovascular operating room nurse) last year, that's when we started working together, but I knew her before that, we had the same shifts and worked with some of the same patients."

"Mrs. Green said she was highly respected, by a lot of medical personnel."

"Oh yeah, Kristin was very intelligent and she was a wonderful nurse, we're all going to miss her." Nick got up now

"Time for round two?" I asked.

"Of course, the cheesecake looks good too!"

Nick made his way to the dessert table, I had finished my breakfast but I thought I would skip dessert for now.

After Nick finished his dessert we decided to take a walk on the ship and look around.

The main lobby and the sun deck were very elegant and resembled a Titanic style in decor.

We continued past the pool deck and came upon a club with music, lights, and a bar, it was crowded with people, dancing and chatting.

"Let's check this out." I suggested to Nick.

We walked in and got a couple of drinks.

We danced a slow dance to Sade's "Lovers Rock"

"I love this song." I commented.

"A Sade fan?" He asked.

"Oh yeah, since the mid-2000s, I think I have every one of her albums on my I phone."

I laid my head on Nick's shoulder, warm and firm muscle with the faint sound of his heartbeat.

He held me close and I knew that our connection for one another was becoming deeper.

After the song was finished we went to our table and finished our drinks.

Looking into each other's eyes we felt like young teenagers flirting and making eyes at one another, innocent and fun.

The next song was a fast one and a throwback to the 70s,

"Macho Man" by The Village People.

We laughed "This song is great." Nick said,

"I have a story for you about this song, in college my roommate dressed up as the construction worker and some of his football teammates wore the other costumes from the band and they go to this party and then they..."

He didn't have a chance to finish his story because we heard a loud yell coming from an older woman on the dance floor.

"Help, someone help, he's having a heart attack."

Nick spared no time he jumped into action, right away saying "I'm a doctor." He shouted, he began assessing the person who fell to the floor grasping his chest.

He told the bartender to call the ship's emergency services immediately. He administered CPR because the patient was suddenly not responsive and no pulse was detected.

He was so calm and confident while using his hands to pump the man's chest with perfectly timed breaths and compressions, the man suddenly opened his eyes and took in a big breath.

He began to speak now, his date or his wife I wasn't sure, tapped at her chest with relief and she began calling out thank you's and thank God from her position by Nick.

Nick asked the man about medications and if he was taking any.

The emergency crew from the ship came running in and they knelt down beside Nick, he told them what happened and something about some kind of medication, and then came some medical lingo that I had no clue what it was.

The music was turned off and the medical team placed the patient on the gurney, and now he was being taken out of the club.

The woman who was with him shook Nick's hand "Thank you, doctor, I'm so glad you were here."

Nick and the emergency team stabilized the patient and we heard a helicopter was called to take the patient to the nearest hospital.

We followed them out of the club and to the heliport on the ship.

The emergency team released the man to the waiting medical team on board the medic flight, and they were off.

Nick and I went back to the ship's lobby, the emergency medic team thanked him and so did some of the other people on board that had witnessed his heroic act, all in a day's work for a heart doctor.

To me, he was my Macho Man, intelligent, skilled, and a hot hero.

"You were amazing, calm, and cool you took charge and saved that man's life, Nick Williams you're my hero!" I hugged him.

He just laughed.

"Any doctor would have done the same."

"You're my Macho Man."

"Ok, I'll take it." He said as I drew him in for a kiss...

Chapter 16

The Elite

I didn't have to tell any of my friends about my date with Nick, it was all over social media and tagged to LINKED TO THE HEART, and to the band's Instagram, plus the social media accounts of Rancho General Hospital and Kendle's.

I had phone calls all morning from all of my friends asking me "What was it like?" and "We want to get to know Nick better."

I didn't have the strength for the gossip today I was more concerned with finding more information about Kristin's death.

Speaking to Nick yesterday gave me an idea for sleuthing.

I put in a call to Mrs. Green.

"Hi, I was wondering if maybe we could speak to some of the nurses at Rancho General about Kristin's relationships with some of the doctors there."

"I spoke to a few of them already but let's go and chat with the nurses that worked with her in the OR, I think they might have a better take on this."

We agreed to meet at the hospital because Mrs. Green had her volunteer schedule today.

The sunshine outside was hot, the weather had warmed to the usual high in the low 90s. Still, with the top off of the jeep, I put my hair in a ponytail and put on a white sleeveless shirt, with a pair of linen pants in light sage green.

I added a pair of platform sandal heels in natural color.

When I reached the hospital I parked the Jeep in the visitor lot and walked to the cafeteria to meet Mrs. Green.

She was sitting at a small table having coffee with two nurses, she waved me over and then introduced me to them.

"Nikki, this is Ella and Janice."

"Nice to meet you two." We shook hands.

They both wore pink scrubs with roses on them, Ella was tall and a redhead, she was Kristin's age, a new mom and wife of just one year. Janice was a few years older, with dark caramel hair and a petite figure, a mom of two, and married to her college sweet heart.

"So you both worked closely with Kristin?"

"We did! We were good friends with her, we talked all of the time we spend so many hours working together it's hard not to become family." Ella replied.

Janice nodded her head yes.

"Can you tell me if she had any run-ins with any of the doctors around here?"

"Kristin got along great with everyone, but she *was* put off by a few doctors. Here at Rancho General, we have a group of them that are like the best in their field, and some of them are nice and professional and some have an elite complex."

"An elite complex?"

Janice filled me in "It's true, there are some that push the envelope and some of them let their expertise get to their heads, it's like best of the best club around here. I've seen it a few times at other hospitals I've worked for."

"Who is in this group?" I asked.

"It's a rumor, but some of the top doctors are on that list and it doesn't mean they are like that but it's more like the popular kids at the table kind of list." Ella said.

"It's like a narcism attitude, they know they are the best and they don't like to be questioned, but like I said not all of them are like that some are just very good at their specialty."

Janice clarified.

"How many doctors?"

"It's about ten or so!"

"Can you put that list together for me?"

"Sure give me your number I'll text it to you by the end of the day." Janice offered taking my number into her contacts on her phone.

"Will I see you both at the funeral?"

"Yes, we will be there!" They both said.

"Maybe if you see some of the doctors on the list there you can point them out to me."

"Sure." they said.

The ladies had to get back to work so we said our goodbyes and I told them I would see them at the funeral.

"If you can find the person who did this, we would all be very grateful Nikki. Janice and I know you have solved other cases here in our town and maybe you can give Kristin justice too!"

"I will do my best." I told them with confidence.

Janice and Ella went back to their floors and Mrs. Green said she would see me later, she went back to the pediatrics floor to finish her volunteer shift.

I was a bit thirsty and this *was* the cafeteria so I decided to grab a bottle of water.

I worked my way through the maze of choices in the beverage cooler until I found a bottle of Fiji water and then I stood in line to pay.

"Hi, Nikki is it?" A thirty-something good-looking doctor said from behind me wearing a fancy blue stethoscope.

"Hi," I managed, not knowing who this doctor was!

"You don't know me, but I'm Dr. Taylor Ferguson."

"Nick's friend." I snapped my fingers guessing correctly.

"Yeah, my best bud, race car winner, and Mr. Hero"

he laughed.

"You heard about the race and let me guess you saw the life-saving

video?" I asked.

"I think everyone did, and that car of his, I've driven it a few times, it's

so freakin' cool!" He responded.

We shook hands and exchanged pleasantries!

"You can say that again, I'm a big fan of it too!"

He had a salad and some fruit on his tray and a cold can of Diet Coke.

"Lunchtime huh?"

"Yeah, I have surgery in two hours."

"That's a pretty fancy stethoscope you have there." I said noticing how

sophisticated it looked.

"I got this last year as a gift from a friend, it's a beauty isn't it?"

"Yes, I like the color and that fancy L on it, does it mean anything?"

"It stands for Lincoln, my high school alma mater."

"Nice." I complimented.

"So are you here to see Nick?" He asked.

"No, I was visiting with Mrs. Green." I smiled.

"Oh yeah everyone loves her here, she's a great gal."

I paid for my water and said bye to Taylor.

"Well, I guess I'll see ya around."

He swiped his badge at the counter and then followed me.

"Hey Nikki, I just want to say that Nick has never been happier, you're all that he talks about."

Taylor told me sincerely.

I smiled deeply "He makes me happy too, I'm so glad I met him."

"Take care, Nikki."

With that, he headed back to the elevators.

I left the hospital and went to work at Kendle's, we were busy and I had so much to do but by the end of the day, Janice sent me that list of doctors, via text:

The Elite Club

Dr. Roger Sanjay

Dr. Derringer Smith

Dr. Todd Matsuda

Dr. Taylor Ferguson

Dr. Raul Mendoza

Dr. Bryan Pratt

Dr. Jack Ungaygupta

Dr. Neal Patterson II

Dr. Dean Markowitz

Dr. Nick Williams III

Nick was on this list oh no!

Chapter 17

"Let's Groove Tonight"

"It's Wednesday and you know what that means? Disco Wednesday!" I shouted into the microphone.

I opened the evening with this exact line as the band and I started our first song of the evening "Let's Groove Tonight" By Earth Wind and Fire.

I had taken great pains to market the heck out of this event, all stemming from the night I was taken out to the Blue 7 club by Martin and Oliver. They had a last chance at trying to cheer me up after my break up with Paul and after Matt left our unbreakable friendship broken!

Tonight was clear and cool, a nice change from the high temps coming on during the day.

This evening I was decked out in my retro 1970s black silk wrap dress. Roxy in black slacks bell bottoms and a strapless silk top, and of course her signature color today a Disco Red lipstick.

The rest of the gals had on the same dress I had on except for Taylor, she dressed up like Roxy.

We were so hip and cool, wow they wore cute stuff in the 1970s, but then again some of it was not so good. Every generation has its good fashion and its oopsies too!

The place was packed and I had done my job in promoting tonight's event. "Ok, folks next we will be having our 1st annual Kendle's dance contest."

We had five couples on the dance floor and now we played the song "If I Can't Have You" by Yvonne Elliman from the Saturday Night Fever soundtrack.

That is one amazing soundtrack!

The dancers moved about showing off their best moves.

I had nominated three judges, Oliver, Sara, and Chef Stark, among the five competitors Craig and Kiana were on the dance floor, and surprisingly Craig could definitely cut a rug.

After two eliminations we were down to three couples, Craig and Kiana being one of them, my old pal, Joanna, and her husband Bob, owners of Coco Jo's Kitchen store, were one of the finalists too and the last couple was from Monrovia.

Each contestant was going to dance to a song on the dance floor all to themselves. First up was the couple from Monrovia, we sang "More,

More, More" By Andrea True. The couple danced and twirled on the dance floor, slow but the moves were solid.

Next, we sang "Lady Marmalade" By Patti Labelle.

Joanne and Bob had the energy and rhythm, they turned and twirled, and boogied on. It was their generation and they hadn't missed a beat in 47 years.

Last but not least we sang "Disco Inferno" by The Tramps for Craig and Kiana. They were moving like pros, Craig even looked like a Pulp Fiction John Travolta. He had the moves and everyone was totally shocked.

"Ok everyone please give a round of applause to the contestants.

The room cheered and clapped for the contestants.

I walked over to the judge's table, Oliver handed me an envelope and I returned to the stage.

"Ladies and gentlemen we have the decision from the judges here."

I held up the envelope and Roxy gave me a drum roll...

"In third place and a winner of a champagne gift basket for the 1st annual Disco Wednesday dance contest, the fabulous Kay and Kevin from Monrovia, Ca."

They came up to the stage and I handed them their gift basket, filled with a bottle of champagne, two champagne flute glasses, and some fine chocolates and nut mixes, and a $150.00 gift Visa card.

"Thank you." They smiled accepting their award.

On the dance floor Craig and Kiana, Joanne, and Bob stood waiting with excitement to find out who will get the coveted mock gold trophy with bragging rights.

"The next couple and first runner-up goes to Joanne and Bob!"

They clapped and yelled and jumped for joy, Craig hugged Kiana, and I took an even bigger basket and handed it to Joanne. Besides the wonderful champagne package, I added two VIP tickets to see Grease at the Hollywood Bowl.

Joanne saw the tickets in the basket, and her eyes grew large, "I wanted to get tickets for that but they were sold out, oh my gosh second place is fine by me. She accepted her basket now with her arms wrapped around it.

"That's great Joanne." I hugged her.

Oliver handed me the trophy and I gave it to Craig and Kiana along with their champagne basket and a weekend in Carmel California, a hotel and spa package.

"This is so amazing, look Craig!" Kiana said with her petite laugh and smile.

Craig was all smiles and enjoyed the accolades coming from the crowd, he was really eating it up.

I went back to the stage and we began another song and I invited everyone back onto the dance floor.

"That's The Way I Like It" by K.C. & The Sunshine Band, we started belting out.

I danced with some of my customers circling the dance floor, and singing to them.

Later on, we went on a break and I headed to the kitchen, we put on the house disco music a montage of greatest hits for everyone.

I had a pitcher of ice water and a small towel for myself in the back.

Sara followed me into the kitchen, "Nikki, I just want to thank you again for letting me have my party here at Kendle's, it's going to be so much fun, I can't wait!

Did you get my mom's credit card information she gave it to the banquet manager, and then she said if you want to add the bar tab, or in my case the soda bar to it that would be fine too."

I think Sara had too many sodas already she was flying through everything she was saying.

"Sara I've got it don't worry." I reassured her taking a long sip of my water.

"You don't have to worry about Matt, I don't think he's all that upset at you anymore. I have been explaining to him the last four months why you covered for me and now I think he understands."

"What do you mean Sara?"

I asked with curiosity.

"I told him the reason why you kept my secret is for the fact that you don't have any brothers or sisters so with me I'm like the little sister you never had and of course, you kept your promise to me that's what sisters do for each other."

She said matter of fact and with authority.

"And he bought that?" I asked her.

"He's coming around, I think deep down he admires your loyalty, plus I told him that he didn't exactly lay claim to you or anything so why is he so sour about your word, it's not like you guys have any commitment to each other, you guys broke up last year right. He thought about that and didn't say anything just walked away."

"Good point Sara."

Chapter 18

Outsmarting An Ape

Last night at the dance contest I wanted to talk to Craig and pick his

brain about the investigation. I got busy last night and before I could

corner him, he and Kiana headed home.

So this morning I thought I could catch him on his way out.

I knew he left at precisely 7 am each morning to get in his workout at

the gym before he had to be at the department at 10 am. He usually

stays at work until 6 pm or 7 depending on his schedule or later if he

has a lead on a case and I wasn't sure I'd be able to catch him at that

time.

I put on a pair of grey sweats and a T-shirt and my white running shoes.

I ran out the door just as Craig was coming down the stairs.

"Good morning Craig, did you sleep well?"

"Oh yeah I feel great, I'm gonna get my workout on, two hours of

upper body today."

"So Craig I forgot to ask how is the case going?" I asked walking with

him toward his car.

He stopped and turned to me, his gym bag in his hand.

"That's right you don't have the low down anymore." He smirked a little.

I ignored his comment and dove right in, "Have you narrowed down the suspect pool?"

"Well!" He said slowly and looked around for witnesses.

"No, but we have a lead on three persons of interest, at the hospital."

"Do they have any association with LINKED TO THE HEART?"

He looked a little surprised "Why would you say that?"

"Just curious." I innocently told him.

"Nikki, If you know something you shouldn't hinder an investigation, you know this."

"No, seriously I asked because Kristin had a brochure about LINKED TO THE HEART, and she was already in a relationship with Donnie Giacomo, so it just hasn't been sitting well with me. Almost like there's something else to it."

He let the thought sink in and pondered it.

"Yeah I see your point, I'll look into it!"

"Thanks, Craig I hope you guys catch the killer soon!"

He walked away now but then came back,

"Hey you know uh we're selling raffle tickets at work for the annual cowboy BBQ at the end of the summer.

What say you take a few tickets off my hands, Nikki."

"Oh no, Craig I'm not buying anything."

"You know Nikki, I always find it a pleasure to share details with you, you know because you're a friend from high school and you're cool people, maybe you can help me too, capiche!"

He said trying to negotiate another scam and looking like the proverbial wicked used car salesman.

I put on a sly face and responded.

"Oh but Craig, I did help you already, didn't you win first prize last night at the dance contest."

"You didn't!" He looked at me in surprise as he raised his hand to his mouth in disbelief!

"Have a good time in Carmel with Kiana, oh, and make sure I get an update later on those police interviews." I smiled and did a two-thumbs-up gesture and went back to my condo!

After I left Craig speechless I decided I needed to look for more information. I still had another unanswered question in my book of clues.

1. *The key pendant from Tiffany's that Mrs. Green couldn't find. What happened to it?*

I sent a quick text to Mrs, Green

Did you ever find the key Pendant Mrs. Green?

I waited a few minutes

Then she replied

"No! Nikki, I still haven't found it! I called Paul and he said they didn't have any jewelry that was with Kristin!"

"Ok, I'll keep looking. Do you mind if I go to Kristins and look around again?"

"Be my guest, but I'm going to the hospital to fill in for a friend, I'll leave you the key, I'll be right down.

Within a few minutes, Mrs. Green dropped off the key to Kristin's apartment. "Thank you, Nikki, for trying to find it, I owe you one."

"No problem Mrs. Green maybe I can find it for tomorrow's funeral, cross your fingers."

"I will thanks again." She left in a hurry.

I changed into some clothes more suited for sleuthing, black jeans, a black T-shirt, and a backpack in case I found anything new. I packed a pepper spray to go with it, and I put on a pair of black sketcher slip-on athletic shoes.

I drove over to Kristin's apartment and parked in a visitor's spot.

I didn't see much activity in the complex, it seemed like it was usually quiet and empty.

I walked to the door and unlocked it, but then I walked into a big mess!

The furniture had been thrown and turned upside down, there were papers and broken glass all over the floor.

The sliding glass door was open, the lock was broken and scratched up.

I pulled out my phone and dialed Paul's number.

"Hi, Nikki." Paul answered.

"Paul can you get to Kristin's apartment, someone broke in."

Paul wasn't too far so he got here in about five minutes.

He was alone today and came in the black charger.

He walked up to me, I was waiting outside the door of the apartment, and I had no idea if anyone was still lurking.

"Is anyone inside?"

"I don't know!" I responded.

He pulled his Glock and went in.

After a few minutes, he came back out and gave me the all-clear.

"Whoever was there is gone now!

What are you doing here?"

He asked in his cop demeanor.

"I have a key, I'm not breaking in, Mrs. Green wanted a piece of jewelry for Kristin for tomorrow's funeral.

It's a family heirloom, and she can't find it, so I told her I'd search the place and see if it turns up."

"Yeah, that's right the key pendant from Tiffany's, she called me and wanted to know if we had it. It wasn't with any of Kristin's things."

We walked back into the apartment, slowly and still going over details.

"I'm going to call and get forensics in here and see if maybe the person who did this left something."

He called for a CSI team, and I walked around but not touching anything.

"Nikki, I need you out of here, can you wait outside."

"Of course."

I walked outside and sat on a bench in the courtyard.

I bet someone was trying to find the flash drive, that's the only thing that makes sense!

The crew Paul called came in and was ready to do a sweep of forensics over the apartment, I figured I couldn't snoop right now, but maybe later.

Paul walked out of the apartment and over to me.

"Thanks for calling me Nikki, it's better that we can go over the place as soon as possible."

"I was with Mrs. Green a few weeks ago when we came to get Kristin's things. So my fingerprints will most likely be here too!"

"Ok." He responded.

Just when I was ready to leave a CSI detective came out to talk to Paul.

"Detective, we found this by the back door."

The officer held up a small vile, with remittance of a white powder substance.

"We tested it, and it's positive for cocaine."

Paul and I looked at one another

"The killer was here!" I said out loud.

Chapter 19

The Godfather

After Paul and I got the news that the killer had most likely been in Kristin's apartment, I went home. I called Mrs. Green and let her know what had happened.

"Nikki, that's horrible, that means the killer was looking for evidence, do you suppose he knew that Kristin was recording him in the locker room?"

"That would be my guess, Mrs. Green."

"Oh dear, ok well I'll see you tomorrow I'm going to call Donnie and tell him what happened."

"See you tomorrow."

I wrote down my clue in my book,

1. *The missing key necklace*

2. *The flash drive*

3. *A vile of remnants of cocaine.*

I closed my book, and I thought about it, the killer must have Kristin's necklace and if he does, maybe he took it for a memento. Why? I thought about it was the killer ever involved with Kristin maybe in a relationship with her? Who was she dating before Donnie Giacomo? Here was another thought. I found the flash drive and I gave it to the police. Kristin had recorded the doctor on her phone and then transferred it to the flash drive. Kristin knew her phone wasn't safe right?

The phone wasn't with the items Paul gave to Mrs, Green and if the department *had* Kristin's phone, they would have found her videos. So then where *is* Kristin's phone?

I called Mrs. Green, and she answered right away.

"Hi, Nikki."

"I had a question for you, did Kristin ever date any doctors that she worked with?"

"She briefly dated a few when she first started working here."

"Who were they?"

"Oh boy let me think, it was about four years ago." She thought for a moment then she said. "Kristin dated Dr. Pattersen and Dr. Mendoza, and a rumor of another doctor but no one knew who it was. She also had a secret admirer last year, but she never found out who that was."

"Ok, I need to look into those two doctors, and the other one seems like a phantom by way of gossip, he probably doesn't exist. I know Paul won't give me any information if I suggest doing a check on them."

"Nikki, call Donnie, he has some contacts that can find some information."

"Ok, I will, I'll talk to you later.

I put in a call to Donnie next.

"Mr. Giacomo can I ask you for a favor."

I told him about checking into these two men, and a secret admirer and he said he would put a private investigator on this asap.

"Do you think one of these doctors is her killer?" He asked me.

"Not sure yet, I just need to find out a little bit more about their relationship with Kristin and I'd like to find out who this secret admirer was!"

"Ok, give me a few days and I'll find something." I asked him if he knew where Kristen would keep her phone when she was working.

"I know she had to leave it in the locker room, it's policy, why do you ask?"

"We can't find Kristin's phone the police don't have it, so my guess is the killer has it."

"What about a trace like a find my phone?" He asked.

"If you can look into that and get a trace we can find where the killer is."

"I'm on top of it Nikki, I'll be in touch..."

I had a craving for a latte, so I headed over to see Jessica.

Starbucks wasn't too busy at this time and Jessica was able to take a break and chat with me for a few minutes.

"Tell me what's new Nikki?"

"I had to call Paul and have him come to Kristin's apartment, someone broke in and they turned the place upside down."

"What! No way."

"Yeah and I think the killer was looking for the flash drive, and I believe the killer has Kristin's phone we can't find it anywhere."

"The police don't have it?" Jessica asked.

"Nope." I shook my head.

"So what's next?"

"Well, I asked Mrs. Green if she knew who dated Kristen in the past and did she date any doctors, Mrs. Green gave me two names and a secret admirer."

"Are you going to tell Paul?"

"No! I have a better way to find this information, I put in a call to Mr. Giacomo and he told me he can have a private investigator look into it."

"A private investigator! Uh Nikki, you don't know much about Donnie Giacomo do you."

"What do you mean?" I asked cluelessly.

She chuckled.

"Nikki, Donnie does have resources, and let's just say he can call the shots."

I looked at her wondering what I was missing.

"What?" I asked confused and scrunching my face in ignorance.

"Nikki, Donnie Giacomo is a nice guy he helps the community, he has respect for moms and grandmothers, he's a giving guy and he does a lot to help people in need."

"He's also a good friend of Chef Stark too!" I added.

"Yeah they went to high school together, they are from the same neighborhood." Jessica replied.

"Jessica, what am I missing?"

"Nikki, come on! Donnie Giacomo is a Godfather." She burst out with certainty.

"Whose Godfather is he?"

"Nikki!" She was growing frustrated "He's like *The Godfather*, you know like the movie." She used her hands to make quotations,

"Oh....." I finally got it!

"So we might see a horse head in someone's bed?"

"He won't be that kind to the killer." She said.

Chapter 20

Channeling Colombo

St. Mark's Catholic Church was packed with many nurses, doctors, medical techs, and many others that worked at Rancho General Hospital. I sat at a front pew with Mrs, Green right by my side, others in the front were Donnie Giacomo, Kristen's Uncle from back east, her cousin, and her two best friends Janice and Ella.

The mass was a traditional one, generally an hour long, with hymns and full communion.

The white coffin with gold handles lay before us, decorated with the pink and white floral spread upon it. Mrs. Green and Donnie decided to keep the casket closed but before the mass, a select few were able to see her.

Donnie kissed her cheek and placed a pink rosary over her hands. Mrs. Green and Kristin's family said their goodbye as well. I was very reluctant to view her but I wanted to get a look at her neck.

The mortuary makeup artist covered her bruising very well, I had to ask Mrs. Green where the L shape imprint was.

She showed me the side of the neck, I rubbed a bit of the makeup and saw that it looked like a capital L but in cursive. I thought of the great TV detective Columbo with Peter Faulk his detective series went from 1970-2003 movie of the week series. He was always so good with small clues that later solved the case.

I studied it for a few seconds, the imprint of the L, and recorded it to memory, I saved it for later...

I looked around the church discreetly and saw the many different faces of her co-workers, I saw Paul, Sonya, and Craig dressed in suits in the back of the church.

Craig had been good on his word and told me about the interview of the three suspects involved, Dr. Mendoza, and Dr. Patterson, the third person was Jazz Montgomery but just as a character witness not as a suspect. The same two doctors we were looking into. He didn't say anything about a secret admirer or a third doctor that had allegedly dated Kristin. He said the two doctors were cleared and no longer on their list.

The mass let out and next, we were on our way to the cemetery, just down the street. I rode in the limo with Mrs. Green, one of Kristin's cousins, her uncle, and Roxy.

Kristin's uncle had stated his two other daughters couldn't be here, one was in the Army overseas in Germany and the other had recently given birth to her second child and was still in the hospital.

They sent their message via video chat with us before the funeral began and told Mrs. Green they appreciated all that she had done for their cousin. They also thanked Donnie for making Kristin so happy before she left us.

At the cemetery, the family sat up front, the priest gave his final blessings, and Kristin's friends were able to say some kind words.

Mr. Giacomo recited a poem for her. Ella and Janice read a passage of inspiration, and Mrs. Green gave a beautiful final speech about Kristin and her parents.

The casket was lowered and we said a final goodbye to Kristin. I had studied the room in the church but no one had shown any odd behavior. I glanced around the cemetery and noticed Nick and Dr. Ferguson standing by five other doctors at the back of the two rows of seated guests outside today. The sunny day had mild temps for noon time, with a light breeze that blew by, along with a few monarch butterflies that made their way, fluttering around Kristin's coffin. After twenty minutes the family tossed pink and white peonies into the grave for a final goodbye.

When the ceremony concluded and everyone walked back to their cars.
Nick jogged to catch up to me.

"Nikki." he hugged me and rubbed my shoulder

"Hi Nick, are you coming to the reception at Cafe Gothic?"

"I can swing by for a while, but then I have to head back I have rounds
to make."

"Ok, I uh, I rode with Mrs. Green, I'll meet you there."

"Ok, sure."

Nick headed off and I followed the family back to the car.

Paul hadn't said anything to me, he just acknowledged me with a quick
wave.

When we arrived at the Cafe Gothic and Inn, the banquet room had
been set up buffet style with round tables for guests to sit at.

The entryway had a photo of Kristin getting her RN from college, and a
small guest book sat by the entry where everyone was signing it and
taking time to reminisce.

The soft music played while people chatted and ate and socialized.
Nick and I sat at a table together, and Roxy and I made sure Mrs. Green
ate something. I didn't see my RNPD friends, they went back to the
station. Paul, Sonya, and Craig had scoped out the church and the
cemetery and most likely came up with zero!

I had a good look at some of the doctors on the list, Ella had come by the table with some of them and she introduced me to seven of the ten "Elite".

They were gracious and they gave Mrs. Green and Kristin's family their condolences.

As I watched them speak and socialize I had a chill, one of these men was a killer, with a drug problem, but I was nowhere close to weeding him out! I wish I had help from someone like Colombo.

Chapter 21

Time to Play a Dating Game

The next day Nick and I were expected to be on the set at 9 am for our review of the date. CeeCee's podcast today was live again. The good news was that it was at the Hampton Hotel right here in Rancho Niguel. If Nick and I agreed to move forward the stakes would be raised and the games would begin.

Nick and I came separately, when I saw him pull into the parking lot he drove over and parked his Vette next to my jeep. He hugged me and then mentioned to me

"Nikki, I need to talk to you."

He sounded serious as if it was something that couldn't wait, maybe something he had to get off of his chest. I was curious but not overly concerned. I figured maybe he was worried about the podcast, CeeCee had a way of making people feel uncomfortable.

"What's going on?" I calmly asked him.

He was ready to go into his speech but then as soon as we entered the banquet room, we were ushered in right away, where the podcast was being held.

We were the second couple to arrive, Jazz Montgomery and his date Denise were waiting as well.

"Hi, Jazz."

"Hi Nikki, how are you?"

"I'm good, how about you two?"

"A little nervous." Denise confessed

"I think it's supposed to be a little more intense today." I replied.

Nick had said we would talk later but he looked a little worried, something was a miss. Right now I had to put on a show so my questions and curiosity would have to wait!

The room was set with four sofas and a spinning wheel to the left. What were we going to do spin for the lottery numbers? Nick and I were up first, we sat on a loveseat together with CeeCee sitting to the right of us. We began right away with the camera gal counting down 3 2 1...

"Here we are ya'll back on my live podcast of LINKED TO THE HEART! Today we have Nick Williams and Nikki Rodriguez, and ladies and gentlemen we get to hear about their date. But before we begin I'd like to thank my sponsor today.

When you're feeling the burn, cool it down with a soothing chamomile butter, brought to you by Big Al's Hemorrhoid Cream."

I couldn't believe CeeCee had a straight face after reading that spiel. "Now gettin' down to business folks, Nick I heard that you saved someone's life on your date?" She was grinning with excitement "Tell us what happened!"

"Yes, a man was having a heart attack but he is doing much better now. I wish him all of the best." Nick said, he was downplaying his act of heroism and made it seem like any doctor would do their service to save a life.

"Oh honey CeeCee saw the footage, you were a hero!" She tapped his knee.

"Thank You CeeCee, I'm glad I was there to help."

CeeCee smiled at Nick and batted her eyes at him.

"Oh so brave and so modest!" She said, then she turned her attention to me. I was just about to say hello, I am here on this couch too you know!

"Nikki, you had a first-hand look at how Nick jumped into action what did you think?" She asked like a gossip reporter for a tabloid magazine. I brushed my opinion of her away and went on to answer her question.

"I have to say it was a very intense moment, but I was so proud of Nick, he saved a life and for me that was it! I think he is a brave and wonderful guy." I turned to him and smiled.

"So for those of ya'll on Inner Tube watching our podcast, here is the footage from Nick's heroic actions."

CeeCee rolled the video and we watched! After the video was over, CeeCee turned to us and asked Nick a question.

"Nick, after your date with Nikki I am going to ask you, Do you want another date with Nikki?"

Nick smiled at me "Absolutely."

"Nikki, would you like another date with Nick?"

"Yes," I replied holding Nick's hand.

For the next half of the show Jazz and Denise moved to the sofa and they told everyone about their second date and agreed to move forward for a third. CeeCee asked Nick and me to come to the color wheel, to spin it.

"Ok, it looks like we have another date for these two as well, now Nick ya'll need to spin the wheel to find out where you're going next."

Nick and I walked over to the wheel and I gave it a spin, round, and round it went with a little red ball jumping in one grade and another until the wheel slowed to a stop.

The dancing red ball stopped at a West Coast Skating rink!

Nick and I looked at each other, "a skating rink?"

I hadn't skated since I was 11 years old, this would be a laughable moment for me.

"The skating rink will be your last date with LINKED TO THE HEART, let's make it the best yet folks." CeeCee replied.

"Now here, we get competitive, Nick you and Nikki will be entering the skating contest against Jazz and Denise.

The twist here is that the four of ya'll will have your date there. Ya'll can go anywhere ya want for dinner, but you must meet up at the rink by 7 pm a week from today! We will have five more of our dating couples there as well, and we will broadcast live for our podcast, so be ready to boogie on in yo skates. This is CeeCee Sass and until next time we will see you at the rink."

We signed off the podcast and now we were finished.

CeeCee hugged the men with gusto and waved to Denise and me.

"Nikki, should we be concerned for our guys?" She pointed at CeeCee who walked away tall and confident. We both laughed

"I wouldn't worry about Miss CeeCee." I replied.

Nick and I headed outside the hotel and to our cars, when we got to the jeep, Nick stopped me.

"Nikki, I have to tell you that I have had two visits from Paul, he wants me to come into the station for more questioning, does he think that I have something to do with Kristin's murder?"

"Why would he think that? You said so yourself that you barely knew Kristin."

"That's true, we were acquaintances, colleagues nothing more!"

"Nick I believe you, when does he want you to go in?"

"This afternoon in about two hours."

"Call a lawyer, just as a precaution. I'll meet you there!"

After I left Nick, I decided to go back to Kristin's place and give it another look.

I still had Mrs. Green's spare key with me. When I arrived the crime scene tape had been removed. I opened the door, and the room was still trashed but now black fingerprint dust was everywhere.

I searched the living room and then after coming up empty I went to the bedroom. I searched the drawers, the closet, the linen closet, under the bed, under the bureau, and also back in the bathroom.

I came up empty. I went to the kitchen and started going through cabinets, cups, salt shakers, spice tins, coffee jars, and even the freezer. Still nothing.

I did find more information about LINKED TO THE HEART. Kristin had put an article about the dating service on the fridge, held up by a yellow flower magnet.

I took it from the fridge and put it in my pocket. I wondered why was Kristin so interested in LINKED TO THE HEART.

Why was she looking into them? I decided to think on it later, I left the apartment and decided to visit Paul, I wanted a reason why he was zeroing in on Nick!

Chapter 22

Not Hawaii 5.0

I drove into the visitor's parking lot at the police station and parked the jeep close to the entrance. I walked in through the double glass doors, where I noticed Paul talking to a teen and telling him to watch out for others the next time he decides to use his bicycle on the walking path at the Rancho Trail.

The teen nodded and apologized for his actions, shook hands with Paul, and headed back out.

Paul smiled at me "What brings you here?"

I put my hand on my hip, no hint of a smile on my face!

"I want to know why you're harassing Nick?"

His smile faded, and he simply said "That's a police matter, it's none of your business."

His cold demeanor returned and now he was back to giving me the attitude. I wasn't going to stand here and allow him to ignore me!

"You're making a big mistake, Nick didn't kill Kristin!"

I demanded.

He turned around and faced me.

"Nikki, I'm following the evidence, that's it! It's not personal."

I came closer to him, so I wouldn't shout.

"It's personal to me, and I'm telling you he's not your guy. He just saved a man who had a heart attack!"

Paul took a step back.

"I know I saw the podcast with CeeCee Sass, look I can't discuss this anymore with you, it's an investigation and I'm just doing my job." He wasn't mad or rude, he was just in official investigator mode.

I moved closer once again and said.

"I can tell you Nick is not on drugs, he barely knew Kristin, they were colleagues, he didn't have a motive!"

I said making my case.

"Nikki, look I understand why you feel this way, but believe me the evidence is saying something different."

"What evidence? Do you have a clear face from the video is that why?" I asked concerned.

"No the video is still in forensics we can't get a good view yet, it's being sent to the FBI, they have more advanced equipment." He politely stated.

"He didn't do it!" I said with ice in my voice.

"Look, Nikki, I..." Paul didn't finish his sentence because

the door to the lobby opened and Nick walked in with a fancy lawyer.

Nick walked up to me "Nikki"

I smiled at him.

"Hi, Nick."

He introduced me to his lawyer.

"This is Nikki Rodriguez,"

We said hello and shook hands.

"Nice to meet you, sir." I replied.

"Detective this is my lawyer, J.T. Baily." Nick introduced his lawyer to

Paul, and he just nodded.

"Nick why don't you two come with me." Paul opened the door to the

offices. "I'll call you when we're done here."

Nick told me.

"Ok," was all I said.

Paul gave me a sympathetic look and closed the door!

I felt better that Nick had brought a lawyer and I was wondering what

did Paul mean when he said he was following the evidence.

What evidence?

I was just going to leave the station when Sonya came out of the office

door. "Nikki, I heard you were here, so I thought I'd save myself a

phone call."

"What's going on Sonya?"

"I have some news about your case."

I followed her back to her office, she closed the door and we sat down.

"The forensics came back with that hair that we found at the scene from the nail gun attack back in February and it belongs to Stacie McDaniels!"

"Sonya what did I tell you, I knew it would be hers." I smiled confidently.

She put her hand up to slow me down.

"Nikki, the thing is I questioned her and because she has been to the community center several times with Mayor CJ, it could have been left at any one of those times. We can't rely on that for proof, she was there on official business at least four times. I'm sorry but we hit a dead end."

"I can't believe this, I know it's her! What about from the explosion, can she be tied to any of it?"

"Not at this time!"

"So that's it! She gets away with it!" I said feeling defeated.

"Now Nikki, we still have some other avenues to pursue. We have here a timeline for the day of the explosion and here is something that I find strange." She had my full attention.

"Stacie claimed to be with Paul having coffee, and I spoke to Paul and he completely gave her an alibi, for the time during the explosion, but the one thing I was puzzled by was the fact that she told him she was coming from a meeting with the mayor. I called the mayor's office and Marge the assistant told me that Stacie had called in sick that day."

I knew exactly what Sonya was getting at, Stacie had time to set the bomb and used her date with Paul to give her an alibi for when the bomb exploded leading everyone to believe she had nothing to do with it!

"You're right she had time to set it up and she could have used her phone to detonate it." I pointed out.

"That's exactly what I'm thinking, but I can't get her phone records, I would need a warrant and right now no judge would sign it."

"I see your point Sonya, and you know something ever since Paul and I broke up, nothing or no one has tried anything, I haven't had any strange calls, no incidents, or sabotage, and no one following me. It's like suddenly it all stopped!"

"Exactly and who is the one dating Paul right now?" She asked

"Stacie is!" I replied.

Chapter 23

Bad Girls

After I left the 5.0 department I headed to work! Kendle's was doing remarkably well, we were busy and reservations were out for at least three weeks.

I walked in and said hello to Sara, she was in the kitchen having a Coke. "Don't worry boss, I'm off duty."

"Sara you're fine, don't worry I'm not a tuff boss."

"I'm glad you're here, come on Oliver and Martin are in the banquet room, we're having a meeting for the final planning with your event coordinator."

She grabbed my arm and we went to the new banquet room. Martin and Oliver greeted me with hugs and my banquet manager slash catering sales rep Paige Montoya filled me in.

I still needed to hire someone to fill the Banquet manager position, Paige was doing double duty and I needed to get her some help.

We were going over the room setup when Matt walked in.

"Hello everyone, Sara asked me to be here for the meeting." He said casually.

"Thanks for coming we were just going over the details." Oliver said.

I waved and he waved back, with little enthusiasm.

Sara was leading the meeting, and planning where her gifts would be and the band, the cake, etc. The rest of us just followed her and gave some input.

Martin and Sara decided the chocolate fountain should be outside, I second that motion because cleaning the patio of spilled chocolate was easier outside.

"I never had a chocolate fountain for my birthday." Matt joked.

"I didn't either." I smiled.

"I am Mom and Dad's only girl in the family." Sara replied joking with sarcasm.

"She's always been so spoiled." Matt whispered to me.

"Usually the youngest of the family is." I told him.

Matt turned to me.

"I want to thank you, Nikki, for giving Sara a job here. She loves it and she is really happy, my folks said to say thank you as well."

"You're welcome, Sara is doing a fantastic job here." I smiled.

We were still outside on the patio, the calm water fountain running softly, the late afternoon sun lowering in the distance.

"Nikki, I just wanted to say that I..." Matt began to say when Oliver came out and shouted that I had a visitor.

"Nikki you're wanted downstairs, Nick is here!"

"Thanks, Oliver. I guess I better go." I told Matt.

"Sure." He put his hands in the front pockets of his jeans and walked inside with me, I turned to him and asked.

"What were you going to say just a minute ago?"

"Nothing, thanks again." He walked on over to Sara and she showed him the diagram of the party.

I walked out of the banquet room and met Nick at the first-floor bar.

"Come up to my office."

Nick followed me to my office and we sat on one of the sofas in the lobby. I offered him a drink, an old fashioned and I got myself a glass of sauvignon blanc.

"So what happened?"

Nick took a quick drink and then said "My lawyer got the cops to back off, they have some kind of circumstantial evidence, a witness stated that they saw me fight with Kristin the week before she died.

I told them that was wrong because she was on a different schedule than I was that week. I didn't even see her for at least two weeks before she died." He took another drink.

"That's all they have?" I asked him.

"Yeah, and also they have another witness that saw my car leave Kristin's apartment around 6 pm two days before she was killed, I told them that's impossible, I was in surgery both days from 3 pm-7:45 pm. They looked into it and my alibis checked out."

"Nick I don't think you have anything to worry about, you'll be crossed off the list of suspects and you can put this whole thing behind you."

"You're right, are you hungry?" He asked with calm concern

I looked at my clock it read 4:45 pm

"Yes, and you've come to the right place."

I called the kitchen and ordered us two chicken parmesans with angel hair pasta and two Cesar salads.

We ate at the coffee table, with the large cushions on the floor, for seats.

"This is the best chicken Parmesan I've ever had."

Nick said enjoying his late lunch, or early dinner.

"Tony is the best cook!" I told him heaving a big piece of chicken parmesan in my mouth, with that wonderful tomato basil marinara sauce he makes.

After our early dinner, Nick had to leave.

"I have an early surgery tomorrow and I have rounds to make tonight, but maybe we could go to Salt Creek Beach and surf and then have dinner in Dana Point real soon, what do you think?

"Sounds like a plan."

We walked out of the private exit from my office, and Nick pulled me close and then he kissed me...

This evening we performed for a room full of the class of 1976. Quite a few classmates from Rancho Niguel High were having their class reunion at the Hyatt tomorrow night and this evening was the kick-off for them.

We started with "Do You Think I'm Sexy" By Rod Stewart. The dance floor was full and the disco ball was spinning with colors of the rainbow dancing about the room.

The bar was busy upstairs as well and every table was full now. Our next song was slow, "Emotion" By Samantha Sang, and backup vocals by The Bee Gees.

Couples on the dance floor held their partners and swayed to the song. I noticed one couple in particular, Stacie and Paul!

I was sure Stacie came here to rub my nose in the fact that now Paul was hers.

She looked at me a few times and smiled. Paul seemed very uncomfortable and steered Stacie as far away from the stage as he could.

He whispered something in her ear and they walked to their table. He had a glass of iced tea and she had a glass of wine, they didn't seem to talk very much, Paul was more focused on his beef stroganoff than Stacie. Out of the corner of my eye, I saw him a few times searching the room. Who was he looking for?

After our song, we sang a faster tune "I Will Survive" by Gloria Gaynor. Next, we played "The Best Of My Love" by The Emotions. We had a few people singing with us at the bar, I guess now we had some fans. When we ended our song, we had cheers and whistles.

"Ladies and gentlemen we're taking a break but we will be back in a half hour."

I went to the bar and drank the ice water that Tito left for me. I walked toward the kitchen but this also meant walking by Paul's table, I was going to go another way but one of my servers had just come out with an order for a table of four. Just my luck!

I kept my eyes looking forward and didn't even look in their direction, but I heard my name called.

"Nikki," The whiny annoying sound that was Stacie's high-pitched voice rang out.

I turned to their table and Stacie waved her hand "I need a new drink, vodka on the rocks please."

She handed me her empty wine glass and dismissed me with a wave of her other hand.

"I'll get your server for you." I said, staying cool and in control.

Paul turned to me,

"Don't worry about it Nikki, Stacie you don't need one." Paul responded.

I wasn't going to be a part of Stacie's outburst again so I went on, but she grabbed me by the arm! She looked up at me now with her scowl and her slurred speech.

"I said I wanted a drink!" She yelled, raising her voice and making a scene now!

I pulled my arm back. Paul stood up and apologized right away.

"I'm sorry Nikki."

He stood between the booth where Stacie was seated and where I was standing.

To avoid any more stares and whispers in the room I whispered to her.

"Dinner is on me tonight, but I need you to leave."

I told Stacie looking at her and never flinching!

Paul pulled out $200 bucks and left it on the table

"This should cover everything Nikki, I'm sorry."

Paul was beyond embarrassed and took Stacie out of the booth.

He took her by the arm guiding her out, but she continued to be vocal.

"I was just asking the *help* for a drink!"

Stacie laughed.

Paul led her out the front doors and I could faintly hear her yell again about not getting her drink.

 I felt embarrassed for him, why would he go back to her?

I went back to the kitchen and got myself some pasta for dinner.

Poor Paul, I felt bad for him.

Chapter 24

Roller Disco

Today I knew I had a big day! The big roller skating date was this evening with Nick. The competition would be fierce now with all of the other couples competing for a trophy to win a marvelous what?

I had no idea what the prize was!

I had practiced some skating moves yesterday and lo and behold I wasn't as rusty as I thought I was. Nick had told me he was an avid ice skater and he had practiced on wheels yesterday and he got the hang of it pretty quick.

We were as prepared as we could be.

We both agreed that for the competition we would have similar attire. We opted for straight dark denim jeans for Nick, and dark denim tasteful Daisy Dukes for me. No cheek showing and a modest length, with a white t-shirt. There was absolutely no way Nick was wearing spandex. His skates in black and mine in white, I opted for the cute and fluffy red pompoms on my skates.

Nick picked me up at my place in the Vette, he complimented me on my attire and how cool it came out.

"Nikki, you look amazing 1970s here we come."

Nick said giving me the once over.

"You look pretty cool yourself." I replied.

We drove over to West Coast Skating Rink, the building still looked the same as it did when it opened back in 1975, or so said the description with photos on the wall in the lobby. A white building with dark wood trim and dark wood shiplap on the side of the building. The entrance a terra cotta tile floor in rust color, with a front desk of formica orange tops and an authentic rotary phone in avocado green. CeeCee's crew was there with cameras, lighting, and tickets were sold to see the competition today.

Nick and I found an avocado green locker and changed into our skates, we put our shoes in a duffle bag with my jean jacket and his sweatshirt, locked the locker, and headed to the rink.

I adjusted my white tube socks with the red stripes I put on to give a more retro 1970s look. I had cropped my white t-shirt and rolled the sleeves, for a more fitted look. I left my hair locks wild and wavy today, it just seemed to fit the whole theme.

We signed in with CeeCee, so we could get our next assignment.

"Ya'll look fabulous, Nick, gimme sum sugar baby!" CeeCee hugged Nick with gusto, next as soon as she saw Jazz she did the same thing! Denise and I just rolled our eyes.

"I'm getting a little tired of Miss CeeCee being so friendly!" Denise whispered to me.

"Me too, I'm glad this is the last date with her looking over our shoulders."

"Right!" Denise replied.

We fist bumped.

Denise and Jazz had opted for black shorts for jazz and a black flowing short skirt for Denise, they wore matching purple t-shirts but Denise cropped hers too and we had matching tops but in different colors. The other couples competing had similar clothing with retro tube socks and shorts like the kind in the movies from the 70s with the piping around the leg. The roller rink had lights on the ceiling, in green, pink, and blue with mirrors all around the main skating rink. The lobby and dining area floor a rust color flat and thin carpet, was in great shape, maybe it was ordered every couple of years because it was in like new condition. The laminate tables and wood and basket weave chairs in the cafe area created a nice 1979 boho look. The wallpaper on the walls pale ivory with broad stripes of brown, mustard, avocado green, rust, and dark blue. Don't worry I didn't forget the large disco ball in the center of the rink above us.

The DJ sat in a tower-style booth just above the rink, he danced and cranked out tunes, like what was on right now, "Funky Town" by Lipps Inc.

CeeCee demanded our attention and her assistants gave us a rundown on the rules of the competition. "Ladies and gentlemen all of ya'll need to be on the skating rink and we will start the games."

We all entered the rink and began skating, six couples all circling front-facing and some backward skating.

The music revved up and soon we were gliding around the rink to "Night Fever" By The Bee Gees. Nick and I twirled and held hands. He was a good skater I had to say, which is more than some of the other couples, that were holding on to the sides of the rink walls, one couple hit the wall and fell, they were fine, they got up and laughed it off.

The DJ stopped the music and on the mic now was Miss CeeCee instructing the rules of the games. I had spotted Roxy and Jessica at the snack bar, they waved to me and I waved back. I looked over at Nick and he smiled at them and waved too!

I was happy to see that my friends approved of Nick and that they were making him a part of our circle of friends.

"Nikki, there's something I have to tell you." Nick whispered.

I smiled, "Right now, is it important?"

"It's about Kristin."

I felt the walls moving in around me and the sound of CeeCee's voice on the mic sounded slow and melted into oblivion. What was he going to say? Did this have to do with the interview with the police yesterday? What could possibly be so important that he needed to tell me now?

"What is it?" I asked.

"I figured it's going to come out anyway, I did know Kristin a little better than I led on. When I first started working at Rancho General we dated for a few months, it wasn't serious, we just didn't have that connection, we were better as friends and we just kinda left it at that. We were very professional with one another, and we generally had the same insights on our patients, she was a really good nurse, and I respected her. I just wanted you to know that, I don't want to hide anything from you."

"Thank you for being honest, is that why they questioned you yesterday at the station?"

"Yes, they found some photos of her and I, we were hugging each other at a wedding, a friend of hers. There were also photos of us at the beach together and one at a friend's BBQ. They wanted to know about our

163

relationship and I told them I had hardly any contact with her over the last year."

"What did they say?"

"They had a warrant for my phone records but I handed them my phone and I told them I had nothing to hide. After about an hour I got my phone back and they said all of my alibis checked out. They cleared me! My lawyer said they had nothing so I was free to go."

"I knew you were innocent." I told him feeling so relieved.

"It feels like a big weight off my shoulders." He exhaled.

"Nick, you said they checked your phone, to see if you had contact with Kristin's phone, did they get her phone records from the phone company?"

"Oh, yes Detective Anderson said they got a tip about Kristin's phone, it was in the lounge under the lockers, they think that it fell out of her purse or her pocket right before she left.

He said it was cracked and broken so that's why they couldn't find it until they went back and did a thorough search."

"I see!" My first thought was that Donnie's investigator tracked it and told the police where it was. I would have to ask Mrs. Green!

I felt like at least I was able to cross Nick off the Elite list of doctors, now I just had about ten more to comb through.

Our conversation came to an end when we were rounded up to begin the games.

"All right, so can I have my couples line up." CeeCee shouted out. Nick and I went to the center of the rink with everyone else and lined up; girls on the right and boys on the left, across from our partners.

We were given small hula hoops with yellow and orange ribbons on them and the object of the game was to toss them back and forth to our partner without dropping the hoops while skating to

"Love Roller Coaster" by The Ohio Players.

All six couples began skating and circling one another and the hoops now went flying and we were in the thick of the competition.

I threw the hoop to Nick and he caught it, back and forth for the duration of the music. Two couples were out already and there were only four couples left.

CeeCee stopped the music and then she upped the game and had us add another hoop. Armed with two hoops to throw back to Nick the music started again.

Around the rink we went, another couple dropped their two hoops and then we were down to three couples left, us, Jazz and Denise, and one other couple. Around we all went again until the music stopped and a third hoop was added.

This time when I tossed the three hoops to Nick and he barely caught them. For another couple though they weren't so lucky and they missed their hoops. So now we were down to just Jazz and Denise along with us. They skated ahead of us and circled the corner, Denise almost lost her balance when she caught her hoops, and Jazz went around the curve too fast, he began to stumble but he recovered quickly!

The lights above were moving and changing colors rapidly, dancing shadows on the walls and the floor, going around and around was now becoming a nauseous experience.

I focused on the hoops in my hand and ignored the blur of people in my vision as I went by.

I tossed the hoops again, and Nick caught them and tossed them back, I caught them just by the ribbons and when I looked over to see Jazz toss the hoops to Denise, she dropped one.

Thank God I thought, now this part of the completion was over!

CeeCee yelled, "Nick and Nikki are the winners of the first round let's give them a hand."

The crowd cheered with delight.

A large board was wheeled out with all of the names of the competing couples, and a star was placed by our names to indicate a win.

The audience in the rink clapped and now I realized how many people were here watching us today, this was a live podcast streaming on social media as well.

Roxy and Jessica cheered, Sara and Jagger were there too. Next, we moved on to round two. All of the couples were asked back to the rink to participate in the next part of the competition.

CeeCee took the microphone again and announced the game rules and how this next challenge would be played.

The next game was a bean bag toss into a basketball hoop, the object was to take your bean bags and toss them into the baskets that were set up on one side of the rink, they were about five feet tall hoops that stood on the rink.

We began the game by tossing and making baskets, this time going around the rink only lasted three go-arounds. We gave it our all but missed one hoop and we came in second place.

Yay!

The third and final game was to have complete trust in your partner, the women were blindfolded and had to skate around the rink without falling or crashing into the wall. I was just relieved we didn't have to do the limbo, surely we would have been out in the first round if that had been part of the games.

Nick guided me by holding my hands and telling me when a corner was coming.

"Just trust me and listen to the sound of my voice. I won't let you fall or hit a wall."

With the music from Brick called "Dazz," playing overhead on the speakers, I let the beat keep me focused and kept time with the rhythm. We skated picking up speed and moving forward, taking turns around the rink seemed like a breeze, I felt at ease and had let myself trust Nick to take the lead.

When we finished our two rounds we had the audience clapping, I took off my blindfold, and Nick and I were the only two on the skating rink. We won the final round!

The music ended and CeeCee congratulated us on our win

"These two have won a weekend trip, a two-night stay at the Hacienda Resort and Spa in lovely Santa Barbara! Congratulations you two."

CeeCee hugged Nick tight and then smacked his bottom!

Nick moved closer to me and hugged me, CeeCee put a hand on her hip and grabbed her drink. She laughed a big laugh and said "That's it for this round of LINKED TO THE HEART! I'll see ya'll next time with all new couples to see if we can make a connection for them. Good night ya'll!"

The camera operators were done and they began to pack it up, Nick and

I rolled over to the table with all of my friends, Martin and Oliver

arrived just before the last game.

"Congratulations." Oliver said hugging me.

Everyone high-fived us and congratulated us.

Nick excused himself for a moment and I sat down for a much-needed

break, Jessica handed me a cold Coke.

"You guys were so good out there, Were you nervous?"

"To be honest, I was terrified!" I laughed.

An order of pizza arrived at the table and we all dug in for a slice. Nick

came back to our table and joined us for pizza. After we ate we all went

out on the rink and skated to "Shake Your Grove Thing" By Peaches

and Herb.

I told Jessica and Roxy about what Nick had told me about knowing

Kristin. "Wow, I can't believe Paul really thought Nick was behind

this!" Roxy said.

"So what do we do now that they found Kristin's phone? How can we

weed out the doctors on the list?"

Jessica asked as we rounded a corner. "I need to call Donnie and find

out if his investigator has any background on the other Elite doctors

and then we can narrow down the list that way."

"I guess that's our only way around it." Jessica said.

At the end of the night, my friends left and Nick and I walked out to his car.

"What a night Nick, I can't believe how much fun this was."

"Oh yeah I feel the same way, and I thought we were finished in the last round of the hoop tossing, but you held on to it. That was cool."

We got in his car and with the top down in convertible mode, we headed back to my place. Nick said he needed to stop and get gas so we pulled into a gas station. After a few seconds, he said,

"I have to go inside, this pump isn't taking cards."

"Ok!"

Nick went into the Shell mini-market and I sat in the car waiting. There were four other cars here and all of the pumps were not taking cards either, because the line inside was now six long.

I unzipped my purse to get out some lip balm, but it fell after not being properly balanced on my knee and everything inside dropped to the car floor.

My favorite pen rolled under my seat, so I opened the passenger door and got out. I knelt outside of the car to look for it when I spotted it.

I realized it had rolled under the seat.

I then leaned in a reached as far under as I could, but while retrieving my pen, something else caught my eye.

I used my pen and I grabbed the item that shined in the dim light that caught my attention.

It was a silver chain with a silver pendant, in the shape of a key, and made by Tiffany & Co.

It was Kristin's missing necklace.

My body froze!!!

Chapter 25

Nick's Place

Nick dropped me off at my place, I knew he wanted to come in but I made the excuse that I was so tired and that we could go for breakfast or lunch tomorrow. So after he left I went and changed into a pair of black leggings, my black slip-on Skechers, and a black long-sleeve T-shirt. I put on a black ball cap and put my hair into a low bun. I grabbed my keys and drove over to Nick's place. I hadn't been there but I saw his address on the police forms the day the attorney accompanied him. He lived up in the hills not far from Matt's house, in fact, I think he lived one block over from Matt's house. I parked the Jeep around the corner put on some leather gloves and walked to his house, it was the second to the last house on the street.

I saw Nick drive into the garage, with the Corvette. He turned off the engine and then pulled out a grocery bag from the passenger side. He must have made a stop at the store before heading home. He went in through the connecting door to the house, and I made my move. I slid into the garage just as the door rolled down and closed! The garage was dark now and I could hear Nick walking around in the house.

I hadn't thought this through, what was my next move? I was breaking and entering, well I didn't break in I just sort of rolled in when the garage was open, but I knew it was some sort of illegal.

I tried the door to the house and turned the nob slightly, the hall was dark so I slowly crept in.

This part of the house led to a large mudroom and laundry room. This door was open, and next to a long hallway that led to the kitchen. I heard Nick go upstairs, as the sound of the floors being walked on was audible.

The kitchen was dark now and the open-concept room led to the large living room and dining area. Everything was very modern, sleek black cabinets in the kitchen, stainless steel appliances everywhere, a grey sofa, modern and low profile.

The dining room had a dark wood table, with the same design, modern simplicity, sleek, very single-guy style.

I looked around the kitchen cabinets very quietly, opening jars and tea tins, I didn't know what I was looking for but I figured I would know if something caught my attention. I came up empty, nothing unusual to be found. I looked around the living room, nothing really here but two side tables next to the sofa, black and sleek with no drawers. The TV was on the wall with an electric fireplace right beneath it. So by this point, I decided to move to the stairs and took them slowly. One by one until I reached the top and I heard the shower being turned on.

I crawled toward Nick's bedroom staying low so he wouldn't see me. The carpet was very soft and plush, high-end beige Berber. Good choice!

The upstairs reminded me of Matt's house, it has much of the same layout! I made it to his room, and I peeked around the corner, he walked into the bathroom so I crawled toward the bed just in time to see him get in the shower. Surrounded by glass walls with one being frosted for modesty while in the shower it hid him from seeing the bedroom. I went to his dresser and searched his underwear, and socks drawer. One of his nightstands had a journal, a tablet, and some wooden boxes with cufflinks in the drawer. The other nightstand drawers were empty, with a small black alarm clock on top.

I didn't find any hidden drugs, or cocaine the drug the killer had been abusing. I searched but nothing came up! I moved on to the walk-in closet, I searched the pockets on his jackets, his trousers, and jeans, inside his shoes, but I didn't find any drugs.

I heard the water turn off and I almost tripped on a gym bag on the floor, as I made my way out of the closet. I caught myself without making any noise. I wanted to run but instead, I ducked out of the room just in time. He walked to his dresser and hit the remote for the TV, the late-night news was on. I was standing in the dark hallway, just outside of his room. The news story of the hour was still talking about Kristin's murder.

Nick stood watching the segment with a blue towel wrapped around his waist. When the segment was over he said;

"No one's going to figure out what happened to her."

My eyes widened, what did Nick mean by this?

Did he play a part in Kristin's murder? Now my body had chills running up and down my arms. I had to get out of here, if he finds me he might snap. Was he the type to do that? Did I really know him at all? I decided to leave now! My mind racing and thinking of so many different possibilities! Maybe he was good at hiding the truth! Here I had believed he was a great guy but maybe I had it all wrong and I was standing here in the home of a killer.

His phone rang and he went to the bathroom sink to get it, I made my way closer to the staircase. I heard him talking to someone saying, "Sure you can borrow my car again." I didn't want to wait any longer now was my chance to get out!

I went downstairs and crept back to the garage. I knew if I hit the switch I would get out but then would Nick see me.

I decided I would stick to the side of the wall. I went to the button and pushed the opener.

The light went on and an alarm sounded off, I rolled under the garage door that was opening up and kept to the side of the house, and I hid behind some bushes.

I heard Nick running down the stairs and into the garage, then I saw that he had on a pair of shorts and stood with a baseball bat in his hand, ready to attack the person he thought was trying to break in.

My saving grace was that he didn't have a ring cam or any cameras around his property, the light from a few neighbors' homes came on, because of the loud ringing from the alarm.

Nick didn't see anyone so he went back into his house and closed the garage, and turned off the alarm.

When the coast was clear I crept in the dark to the next street to my Jeep.

I got in and drove over the next block before I put my headlights on. My adrenaline was at warp speed now as I drove fast down the hill! After finding Kristin's key pendant in Nick's car I had gone on this mission hoping to prove I was wrong about him but now I didn't know what to think, was he guilty of murder or was he being set up? Either way, I needed the truth.

Chapter 26

I'm Coming Out, With clues

The next morning the sun was shining bright and warm and I still hadn't decided what to do about the necklace.

I kept tossing and turning all night trying to make sense of what I saw and heard last night. I thought of telling Mrs. Green but I knew she would just run to Donnie and then he would kill Nick, I didn't want that to happen.

I came up with the most sensible thing I possibly could I decided to tell Paul!

I sent Paul a text message;

"Hi, Paul,

I have some information about Kristin's murder,

can I meet you at my office as soon as possible?"

He responded quickly.

"I'll be there in an hour."

"See you then." I replied.

I got out of bed and showered fast, dried my hair, and got dressed, I put on a pair of white jeans and a yellow linen blouse, I added some gold hoops, and slid on my Toms wedge heel canvas closed-toe shoes in taupe.

I grabbed my yellow and white striped Dooney and Bourke drawstring sack and went out to meet Paul at my office.

I opened the back door when he knocked, he looked so cute dressed in a pair of jeans, canvas classic vans in navy, and a white Billabong t-shirt with blue waves on it.

"Hi," he smiled with those eyes of his that I adored.

"Come on in." I beckoned him in and we went upstairs to my office.

"It's nice up here." He said taking a seat.

"Would you like some coffee?" I offered.

"Sure."

I poured two cups from the French press I had made right before he arrived, we sat down on the sofa with the coffee table in front of us I placed the two coffee cups down for us.

"So you want to tell me what this is about?" He asked point blank.

The look on my face was sad and a little disappointed,

I picked up the white jewelry box on the table, took off the cover, and showed him the contents, the key pendant necklace!

"Last night I found it in Nick's car under the seat."

He looked surprised to see it, he told me "Did you touch it?"

"No, I used my pen to pick it up and toss it in my purse."

"I'll need to dust it for prints. Tell me how and right from the start."

He asked taking the box from me.

I went over my story about how we stopped for gas, Nick went inside to pay because the gas pumps weren't taking credit cards, and then I dropped a few things out of my purse and I had to open the car door to search under the passenger seat for my items.

I told him I should be on the cameras from the gas station doing exactly what I'm telling him I did.

He listened intently and didn't say anything until I finished my story.

"Ok first thing I'll get this to the lab and then I'll get the cameras from the gas station.

Nikki, I need you to stay away from him until I know what all of this means."

He stood up, finished the last of his coffee, and then told me;

"Look about the other night with Stacie, I just can't tell you how sorry I am."

"Don't worry about it Paul, really. Right now I'm having a hard time with all of this."

I said now looking down and feeling very foolish.

"Nikki, I'm sorry all of this is happening to you."

179

"Thanks," I said with genuine appreciation for his kindness.

After Paul left I put in a call to Roxy.

"Hey girl what's new?" She asked.

"Roxy you're not going to believe this!"

In fifteen minutes Roxy was at my back office door.

I let her in and we talked over bagels and cream cheese that she brought over.

"You didn't tell Paul you went into Nick's house did you?"

"No way, he'd take me in. I'm only telling you what I saw and what Nick said right after watching that news report.

He said, and I quote "No one's going to figure out what happened to her."

I had a chill when I repeated it to Roxy.

"Nikki you need to be careful, I mean, we thought Nick was a stand-up guy, how could we have been so wrong?" She contemplated.

"I don't know but I feel like I'm missing something, I can't figure it out!"

"Didn't you say that Nick told someone it was ok to borrow his car?" Roxy asked.

"Yes, but I have no idea who he was talking to."

We hit a dead end again and came up with nothing, I switched the subject and told Roxy about the other night the incident with Stacie and Paul.

"She called you the *help*, wow that sucks! I saw you talking to them at the table but I didn't stay for the rest I went back to the kitchen to eat." Roxy wasn't surprised by what I told her!

"Yeah, I felt really bad for Paul. Obviously, Stacie has a drinking problem!" I continued to tell her.

"After hearing that I agree. Poor Paul what is he thinking dating her!" Roxy said.

My phone chimed "The Hustle" It was Mrs. Green.

"Hello!"

"Nikki, I have some news, can we talk?"

"Sure Roxy is here." I placed the phone on speaker.

"Hi, Roxy."

"Hey there, you have new info?" Roxy asked.

"Here it goes kids, last night I met with Donnie and his private investigator and we covered some news about Dr. Mendoza and Dr. Patterson."

"What did you find out?" I asked full of curiosity.

"Dr. Patterson was out of town the night Kristen was murdered and he's engaged to be married, he doesn't have a history of any drugs, and he was in surgery during the time that Kristen took the video.

That leaves him out of the lineup, next, Dr. Mendoza is a reserve Marine and he has one year left of his contract they test him regularly for drug use as per regulations for the Marine Core, he never knows when they will drug test him and he's clean, always has been, and he was out of town at a conference in Montana, he was a keynote speaker with 200 witnesses when Kristen was killed.

We're back to square one Nikki, the investigator couldn't find anything else, no secret admirers, except for the fact that Kristin had one, according to all of the gossip at the hospital.

We also found the signal for Kristin's phone and we let the police know where it was, turns out it was in the lounge locker room."

I knew I was right about that.

"Mrs. Green I think the police will have something soon, Paul has had some new evidence surface, and from what I heard they are checking it out."

"Oh, I hope they find out who the culprit is soon!"

"I'll keep you posted Mrs. Green."

Chapter 27

"Nancy Drew"

A few days later Paul called me to tell me about the Key pendant necklace, no prints were found, only a partial and it wasn't enough to get an id on!

He said they swabbed for DNA and the results would be back in another couple of days, that was with a rush on the testing, thank you to Ms. CJ Grooves who is pressing Paul for an arrest.

She has been asking for daily updates, as well as putting a lot of resources into the case. I figured it also had something to do with the fact that she was a friend and an ally to Donnie Giacomo.

Paul had also told me to keep my distance from Nick until we had some absolutes.

Part of me agreed, but another part of me just wasn't 100% sure that Nick had anything to do with it. I had never once seen him look or seem like he was on cocaine.

During the time I spent with him, I never once felt unsafe. Ok well maybe when I found the necklace in his car and then when I was sneaking around his house.

Other than that I just couldn't come to believe that he had anything to do with Kristin's death.

I needed to do more investigating, I had an idea about where my next bit of information would come from, I decided to go to the Hampton tomorrow evening, another speed dating event was going on and I needed to talk to a fan...

I dressed in a pair of black slacks and a white silk tank top with my black strappy heels.

The event this evening wasn't for another 20 minutes so I figured I had enough time to go and find Tory, the gal that checked in all of the bachelors and bachelorettes for the event.

Tory was sitting at her table in front of the banquet room doors. She was checking off names on a list and writing out name tags.

A small laptop sat to her right along with a large Iced Carmel coffee with whipped cream.

"Hi, it's Tory right?"

She looked up from her tasks

"Yes, Hi Nikki Rodriguez, how are you? I went to Kendle's last night oh my gosh it looks so cool, my boyfriend and I had a very romantic dinner on the new patio."

"I'm doing well and I'm glad you both enjoyed yourselves, I just had a question, it won't take up too much of your time."

"Sure what is it?"

"Tory, I was wondering, did Kristin Cabela ever sign up for LINKED TO THE HEART?"

She thought about this, then she went to her laptop and typed away for a few seconds

"No, she never registered here, but she did inquire about another person. I think I have it here in my notes.

I add notes to every call that comes in, it's just my way of CMA you know (Cover My Ass) I've had other jobs where I learned that it was the best way to keep from being fired, you know people make stuff up when they call us and sometimes they accuse us of making guarantees and we could be sued so we record the calls and I place notes on the calls we get.

Here it is, she wanted to know if Dr. Taylor Ferguson was going to be a contestant."

"Did she say why?"

"No, but I told her he said he was inquiring about us for his friend Dr. Nick Williams, your match."

"Yes, that's what I thought Tory thanks I owe him a big thank you!"

"You're welcome, good luck with Dr. Nick, you got a good one there."

"Thanks, Tory, I'll see you."

Walking away from the hotel lobby all I could think about was the fact that I figured out who the killer was but now I had to prove it.

I drove to the station and I hoped I could catch Paul, I walked in and had him paged.

He came to the lobby door and looked happy to see me, I think?

"Nikki, what can I do for you?"

"I need to talk to you." I said sounding urgent.

"Come to my office."

We walked back to the offices until we got to his office, he closed the door behind us.

"Did you find anything new?" He asked.

"I just came back from speaking to Tory, she's the gal at the LINKED TO YOUR HEART event at the Hampton hotel, I asked her if Kristin was going to be a contestant on LINKED and she said no but get this, Kristin wanted to know if Dr. Taylor Ferguson was going to be a contestant."

"Why would she want to know that?" Paul looked a little confused

"It all fits, you see Kristin was following Dr. Ferguson, she knew that he was abusing cocaine, so she decided to record him in the locker room using the drugs. She knew his surgery schedule and she knew when he would be in the locker room. She figured if she could confront him in a public place, exploit him so to speak, she would be safe. When she found out that Dr. Ferguson had signed up Nick to be part of the event, she had to change her plan. Plus Dr. Ferguson has borrowed Nick's car a few times, and Nick was in surgery when he did!"

"Ok, how do you know he borrowed Nick's car did he tell you?"

"Dr. Ferguson said he had driven it a few times when I met him, and Nick told him just the other day he could borrow his car when he was on the phone, that proves it!" I came to the realization of my theory.

"That's who Nick was on the phone with, that night!" I said out loud.

"What are you talking about Nikki?" He looked at me confused by my mumbling.

"The night I was at Nick's house, he had just come out of the shower and his phone rang, I didn't know whom he was talking to I could barely hear his conversation, because I was in the hallway.

That had to be why I found Kristin's necklace in Nick's car!" I was pacing back and forth, my mind was racing through the scenario, trying to put the clues together.

187

"Why didn't you just ask him when he got off the phone who he was speaking to!" Paul had some ice in his voice now.

"He didn't know I was there, I..." Oh darn in my lull of putting the facts together, I had slipped up! I covered my mouth with my hand, I was caught!

Paul looked at me surprised.

"You broke into his house! We got a call from him telling us someone tried to steal his car, but it was you, Nikki! You left from the garage." He put it together now, his slight chuckle coming in low.

I sat down in the chair across from his desk.

"Guilty as charged!" I said admitting to my snooping.

"Tell me everything!" He scolded.

I told him how I got in the garage and waited until he was in the shower to go snooping around his room and closet. I told Paul that I didn't find any drugs or anything that would incriminate Nick.

Then I told him every word of the phone call I heard and also what Nick said when he was watching the news on TV, I told Paul that was when I decided to get out and fast!

Paul was going over my testimony and taking notes to make sure he didn't miss anything.

"You know the first time I met him, Dr. Ferguson, he did seem a little wired, and the stethoscope he had on, it has an L on it!

He told me it was his high school alma mater!" I put my hand up to my mouth in complete shock!

"The murder weapon is the stethoscope!" I shouted out!

"You're right! The letter left on Kristin's neck was an L in cursive." Paul remembered.

"That's what he strangled her with!" I told him.

"You saw it around his neck?"

"Yes!"

"That's what we were missing, A murder weapon!" Paul concluded.

He took out his cell phone and made a phone call.

I looked around his office, it was tidy and organized, but that was Paul, his desk just had his laptop, some notebooks and a cup with pens and pencils, a few picture frames, one of his buddies, one of his family, and one of us holding each other on the dance floor at the Christmas party last December.

I was surprised to see it on his desk, it made me smile.

"Ok, so here's what's going to happen!" Paul laid out a plan.

"I don't want you to repeat what you told me to anyone."

"Roxy knows."

"Ok, anyone else from here on ok Nancy Drew."

"Deal." I replied giving my scouts honor sign with my hand.

"First things first, I called Craig to get Judge Malloy on the phone and get two warrants, one to search and print Nick's car, so we can prove Taylor has been in it, and one to search Taylor's house and take that stethoscope of his and run DNA on it.

I'm going to pull Nick in and get his side of the story about his buddy. I'll bring in Taylor and question him as well and If you're right then Taylor is our killer!"

Chapter 28

You Have The Right

To Remain Silent

I went home after leaving the police department, Paul had his hands full with the searches, and the possible arrest. He said he would fill me in and keep me updated.

He also told me to still keep my distance from Nick until this thing blows over. I couldn't tell anyone and it was hard keeping all of this to myself.

I changed into some pink cotton sweat shorts and a white tank top, to relax and veg in front of the TV. I had the back patio door open to get some fresh cool summer air and luckily I had recently added screen doors to my double French doors, the fewer mosquitos the better.

It was 8 pm and I was starving. I went to the fridge and made some dinner, and a half hour later I was eating a chicken salad sandwich on a buttery croissant, with a bag of potato chips and a cherry Coke.

I turned on the TV to Kid Retro, tonight they had a Three's Company marathon.

One of my all-time favorite comedy sitcoms from the late 1970s-1980s. Suzanne Somers, Joyce De Wit, and the late great John Ritter, two girls, one guy, and lots of innocent shenanigans, not to mention the nosy landlords the Ropers, and the shoddy used car salesman neighbor Larry. I was laughing at these episodes so much that it hurt. Comedy can always soothe the soul. I stayed up watching until maybe midnight and I fell asleep in bed.

The next morning the sun shinned bright in through my white curtains. I took a shower and dressed in some denim shorts and a red and white striped T-shirt. I put on my white platform Keds I just bought for the season, I still hadn't worn them yet.

I opened up the back patio doors to let in the fresh morning air and sunlight.

I had just finished brushing my teeth when I heard a knock at the door. I went to look at the ring cam and I saw Mrs. Green standing there. I wonder if she heard about the search that was going on last night at Nick's place and Taylor's house.

I opened the door with no worries.

"Mrs. Green is everything ok?" She looked very worried and scared.

"Nikki..." she trailed off before being pushed into my place by Taylor with a gun to her back.

"Taylor, what are you doing?" I yelled as I was pushed back into my own living room.

"Shut the door, and if you scream I'll take you both out!" Taylor said pointing the gun at both of us.

"Mrs. Green, what happened?"

"He showed up at my place saying there was an emergency and then he yanked me out of my condo and brought me down here, he said if I didn't cooperate he would kill me!" Mrs. Green said tearing up now.

"Nikki, what are we going to do?"

Taylor had closed my patio door and checked to see if my windows were locked. He looked sleep deprived and cranky, it was undeniable he hadn't slept the entire night. He probably ditched the cops and now was contemplating his escape plan.

"Mrs. Green please just do what he says, he's the one who killed Kristin."

Mrs. Green was horrified!

"He did what? Why?" She shrieked!

Mrs. Green looked at Taylor, with so much contempt.

"Why did you kill Kristin? Why?" She made fists in the air demanding an answer.

193

Taylor had the gun still in his hand, he had been pacing back and forth in the living room. He raked his hand through his blond hair and then sat on a bar stool.

"Because she was going to get me fired and take my medical license, that bitch!"

Mrs. Green was searching for clarification or reasoning in her mind, she sank into the sofa and covered her face with her hands, distraught and in disbelief she sobbed.

"So it's true, you took cocaine before you performed surgery?"

I asked him point blank!

"I just took a small line or two before my surgeries. It was no big deal I had it under control! I just needed a little more energy and it kept me on my game, my surgeries always came out perfect, and I'm an elite doctor with many awards and accolades from the medical board! I saved lives and performed miracles.

I tried to reason with Kristin, I offered her money, I told her I could make her head nurse, I even told her I was her secret admirer, who sent her flowers and theatre tickets and boxes of candy, I loved her!" He shook his head as he was looking back, thinking about why she hadn't just gone ahead with his plan.

"I told her we could rule the hospital the two of us the best of the best, but no, she just turned me down! Me Dr. Taylor Ferguson, I'm a God at

194

Rancho General! How dare she question my judgment and my medical expertise." He stood pumping his fist in the air.

"So you just killed her! Didn't you take an oath to save people not kill them!"

He calmed down now and his face sank a bit.

"I didn't want to hurt her, I swear but that night when we were taking the elevator to the parking garage, I begged her to change her mind, I told her she could name her price, but she laughed and told me if I didn't leave her alone she would tell Donnie I was harassing her." He stopped talking for a minute remembering something then he spoke again calm and straightforward.

"Everyone knows Mr. Godfather, he would have cut my throat and she wasn't going to let this go, she was already going to the board, she said she had proof of what I had done.

So when she walked to her car I followed her, I had to stop her, I just had to!" His anger now resurfacing, with sweat on his brow!

"After she fell to the ground, I took her phone and ripped her necklace off, and slipped out of the garage unseen by anyone.

I thought I was home free until the two of you started asking a bunch of questions."

He stood angry with evil careening eyes now looking at me and Mrs. Green. He still had the gun in his hand and dangerously his finger was on the trigger. I tried to stay out of his line of sight.

"You're not going to get away with this" Mrs. Green yelled as she stood up from the sofa.

"The police have all of the evidence on you and I'm sure the stethoscope will have Kristin's DNA on it." I told him.

"That's where the two of you come in, your both my ticket out of here! Hand me your phone, Nikki!"

"It's in the kitchen."

I pointed to where it was sitting by the sink, Taylor walked to the sink to retrieve it but kept the gun on me, and then handed me my phone.

"Call your cop boyfriend."

He demanded pointing his gun at me once again.

· I dialed Paul's number and he picked up on the first ring

"Hello."

"Paul!" I yelled franticly.

Taylor grabbed the phone from me quickly.

"Listen, cop, I've got your girl and Mrs. Green, and if you don't do what I say you'll be going to their funeral."

Taylor put the phone on speaker mode.

"Taylor let's talk, Why don't you come in and we can get your side of the story? I don't want them hurt." Paul told him.

"I'm not coming in, I want to leave the country, I want a chopper to pick me up at a secure location and then I'll let Mrs. Green go, Nikki stays with me until the chopper gets me to a private jet and as soon as I get on and wheels are up I'll let Nikki go!"

I knew Paul and most likely he sent a 911 text to Craig and Sonya, I knew he was also planning his next move.

"I'm going to have to call my superiors I don't have the authority to grant that, let me call the Mayor." Paul asked.

"Fine, you have an hour, otherwise Mrs. Green and your sweetheart are in the morgue." He hung up my phone and left it on the kitchen counter.

I knew Paul would trace my phone and know that Taylor had us here at my place.

Taylor was pacing again, back and forth thinking of his next move. I had to keep him here long enough for Paul to get some help here.

"Does Nick know what you did?" I asked him.

Taylor stopped pacing, and he sat down again on a bar stool, with the gun still pointed in our direction but lowered now.

"NO! He would have had me turn myself in, Nick is a good guy, he doesn't know anything!"

"Don't you know how hard this will be for him, seeing this happen to you, knowing what you did!"

Taylor looked as though he was contemplating this.

"He's always been a good friend, Nick will understand he's an elite too, he knows what kind of pressure we have on us to be perfect at what we do, people depend on us, he'll understand!" Taylor repeated.

"Nick may forgive you, but he doesn't understand." Mrs. Green shouted out "You're just a coward!"

"You murdered Kristin!" I told him.

"You need to pay for what you did Taylor." Mrs. Green spat back.

He was angry now because we were tag-teaming him with the guilt he should have felt. He then got up and yelled.

"Get up, we're leaving, we're sitting ducks here. Come on let's go!"

Mrs. Green walked toward the front door and I followed as we were ushered out of my place, Taylor had my keys, he tossed them to me, "Drive."

I locked my front door with a gun to me and Mrs. Green. I contemplated trying to hit Taylor but I didn't want to risk him shooting one of us. I had to be smart and try another way. We began walking past the courtyard when a SWAT team came towards us. Mrs.Green and I were startled!

Tactical uniforms and guns at the ready, with Craig, Sonya, and Paul behind them. Taylor put the gun to my waist and held Mrs. Green's wrist to keep her from running.

"You're surrounded now let them go." Paul shouted!

Taylor knew his options were fading, he tried to back up but he was greeted by more SWAT team members coming from behind us.

"You're out of options Taylor, let them go!" Paul shouted!

Taylor looked up and around the courtyard. I looked up and spotted a sharpshooter to my right. This was it! He had no place to run.

He let go of Mrs. Green's hand, but he pulled me with him as he walked backward, the SWAT team and the cops followed him circling us.

A SWAT cop pulled Mrs. Green out of the vortex and took her out of the complex. Taylor had me in front of him. "Stand down now or she gets a bullet to the kidneys."

"Bring it down, guys." Paul said giving the order.

SWAT lowered their weapons, and now Paul walked toward us, "Let's talk Taylor, you don't want to hurt Nikki, just let her go and we can have that chat, tell us your side of the story." Paul was reasoning trying to talk him off the ledge.

Taylor was sweating hard now, he was losing his reasoning and now was running on empty and considering his options.

"I wanna get outta here!" He looked side to side and up to see all of the officers in position, he knew he was not getting out alive if he didn't surrender.

"Ok, let Nikki go and we'll get you out of here. How about this, I'm putting my gun down, take me and let Nikki go."

Paul put his gun on the floor and walked with his hands up to Taylor and I.

Taylor thought this through, Paul was within arms reach now. I wasn't sure what Paul was going to attempt to do but I knew he would do it to save me.

Taylor backed up pulling me with him. Paul followed us and so did the other officers.

Taylor's grip on the gun relaxed and then he turned to me, "Nikki, tell Nick I'm sorry, I didn't mean for any of this to happen."

He surrendered and dropped the gun to the floor and put his hands up. Paul cuffed him and Sonya pulled me out of there. I could hear Craig in the distance.

"You have the right to remain silent..."

Chapter 29

Truce

I danced in the kitchen to "And The Beat Goes On" by The Whispers.
Will Smith remade this song and called it Miami.

I had the TV tuned in to Pandora on a Disco station, while

I made two six-egg Denver Omelets, with some home fries, and I cut

up some fresh fruit. I danced around to The next song by K.C. and The

Sunshine band "Get Down Tonight."

My doorbell rang Mrs. Green came in with some orange juice and

champagne, and Roxy brought in some pastries, danishes, and

doughnuts.

"Go ahead set it on the table the others should be here soon.

In about twenty minutes Oliver, Martin, Jessica, Tito, and Daisy were

sitting at the table with us having breakfast.

"I can't believe it was Dr. Taylor Ferguson, how did you figure this out,

boss?"

Tito asked me.

I filled everyone in on how I put the two together when I was at Nick's house and about speaking with Tory and the information she gave me and then going to Paul with everything I had.

"Nikki, that must have been scary being in Nick's house and not knowing if he was involved."

Daisy remarked.

"Yeah, I agree how did you not get caught?" Martin asked taking a bite of his omelet with cheddar cheese stretching from his fork.

"I have to say I was very scared, but I just kept quiet Nick was distracted with his phone call, but I was worried about getting out of the garage, I thought I would have gotten caught for sure but I just figured I was already in this knee deep."

"Nikki you constantly shock me." Oliver stated.

"I second that!" Roxy lifted her glass.

"Mrs. Green you and Nikki were two tuff chicks, held hostage, and then the scare of being in the middle of the SWAT team, what a story." Jessica said raising her glass.

We toasted to surviving.

"So what happens next for Dr. Taylor?"

Tito asked.

"For one thing he tested positive for cocaine, and they found his stash in his small wall safe at his house. Plus he's been denied bail and his court date is in a week! He has a fancy lawyer from back east that came in for the arraignment and I heard he's pleading not guilty." I took a drink of my mimosa.

"I bet that matches the stuff that was in the vile, that the police found at Kristin's." Martin stated remembering the information from one of the clues we had.

"So what's going on with Nick?" Jessica asked.

Everyone's eyes were on me waiting for the gossip.

"He's taking this pretty hard, Taylor has been his best friend since college and he feels a little guilty for not knowing what was happening to him.

Nick just said he was so busy with work that he never gave it a second thought that Taylor had a cocaine problem."

"Are you guys still seeing each other?" Daisy wondered and so did the rest of them. The room was quiet now as the song was changing.

"Yes, of course, but I'm giving him time to sort this out, I told him to call me when he can."

No one said much after that about my relationships, we began chatting about Kendle's, the dance contest, the new menu, and how wonderful the place looks.

We cleared the table, Jessica and Roxy singing the song "We Are Family" by Sister Sledge.

We grabbed some wooden spoons and sang as a group, dancing around and everyone else clapping to the music.

We sang a few more songs after we cleaned up and laughed about the latest reels on social media.

After everyone left I called Nick.

"Hi, how are you doing today."

"I'm keeping busy at work making rounds and avoiding everyone's whispers, you know there's the best friend of a murder!

that kind of stuff."

"Would you like me to come over later and bring you some dinner?"

"I would love that but honestly I'm so tired I think I'm going home and I'm going to sleep, I decided to take next week off, I need a break."

"That sounds good I'm sure we could maybe catch some waves, there is nothing like surfing for stress relief." I told him.

"That sounds great, I'll take you up on that."

"Ok, it's a date."

"Ok, I'll talk to you soon..."

After I hung up I had a knock at the door, I wonder who that could be. I looked through the ring cam and saw Paul. I opened the door with a smile.

"If it isn't my hero."

He smiled, he must have been off duty, he was in navy blue board shorts and a light blue Hobie T-shirt.

"Would it be ok if we talk?"

"Come on in."

"So... What is this about?"

"I need to clear something up."

"Oh, ok sure." We sat down on the sofa

"Would you like anything to drink?"

"Oh, no thanks I'm fine. I wanted to clear up the rumors that are circling like sharks around here."

"About what?" I asked him wondering what he was talking about.

He thought through his words as he usually did, he always said exactly what he thought and was always honest with me.

"I'm not dating Stacie, I'm her AA sponsor, I'm trying to get her to stop drinking."

"I didn't know." I was shocked to hear this news.

"Yeah, no one does, but everyone has assumed that we're a couple."

"Paul that's your business, you shouldn't have to explain anything to anyone, despite the town gossip."

"I know, but it's important that you know the truth."

I was a little speechless, to say the least, he only cared about what I thought. Why did he break up with me then? Why did he stay away and give me the ice-cold shoulder for four months if this was bothering him?

"You're wondering why I didn't say anything sooner."

"Yes, I am wondering why, you kept your distance."

He sat sideways on the sofa facing me, he looked me in the eyes and told me his side of the story.

"That day that you were injured in the explosion, I guess I got a little possessive and I didn't like Matt being there and I let it get to me. The truth is I should have told you sooner how I felt about him always being around. I broke up with you because I was angry at you! After I ended our relationship, I thought for sure you and Matt would get back together. Then Roxy told me what happened between you and Matt, that he was so upset when you lied about having Sara with you. The rumors were already building about Stacie and me dating and I saw how it affected you, and I wanted you to feel what I felt every time Matt was hanging around you."

"You wanted to get revenge! It worked!" I confessed as I looked into his eyes.

"For that I'm sorry, I shouldn't have done that! It was childish." He admitted.

"I can't believe you're telling me this, I moved on, I tried for four months to communicate with you and you ghosted me. And now I'm in a relationship with someone else"

"I know, but I wanted to be honest with you."

"So where do we go from here?" I asked him.

"Truce."

"Truce"

Chapter 30

It's Party Time

Paul left after about an hour, we didn't make any plans or changes, we agreed on a truce and to be kind to one another. I wasn't sure if he still had feelings for me romantically we didn't go into that but we agreed no more revenge plots or cold shoulders, no more making the other jealous!

Paul said we should be friendly, and no one needed to know the truth. I did admire him for trying to help Stacie, she did need to get help. I knew he had taken a lot of embarrassment in the process of helping her too! I just didn't understand why he was still so loyal to her!

My day today was going to be busy it was Saturday and the big party for Sara was this evening. All of the vendors for tonight were coming in to set up at around 4 pm. I decided to go in at 3 and take a long morning to catch up on some rest.

Sara's guest list came out to 100, right at the cut-off that her parents allowed. Diane and Griffin Stevens were not going to be at Sara's party, this evening, they had given her more freedom because of the great job she was doing at work and the fact that her end-of-the-year GPA was a 4.1 helped her to secure some breathing room from her mom and dad.

I went shopping with her to find a perfect dress, for her 70s disco-themed birthday bash. She found a black beaded spaghetti strap, pleated maxi dress, the top portion resembled a bikini top style.

I opted for a black silk bell bottom jumpsuit, with a halter top and just a little cleavage showing.

We also decided on a DJ, for the party, two of the girls in the band were going to be out of town and I needed a break. I offered to sing one song, with Roxy playing the piano for the dance with Sara and Jagger.

For the most part, I was a guest and a chaperone. Diane had called me last week and asked If I could just keep an eye on these kids, I agreed, and I told her I would watch Sara as if she was my own. "I knew I could count on you, Nikki." Is what she said

I checked in with Chef Stark in the kitchen and everything looked perfect.

Sara, Tony, and I went over the menu, and we decided on

A sit-down dinner of wagyu burgers or garden burgers (a vegan and a carnivore option) with cheese, lettuce tomato, and condiments at the table. Seasoned shoestring fries and then a buffet of snacks after.

For the buffet of snacks, we had two varieties of popcorn, butter, and Carmel, a cotton candy station, a nachos station, BBQ chicken skewers, flat bread mini pizza, small hoagie sandwiches, turkey, roast beef, veggie, and Italian. We added a candy bar with a variety of mini candy bars and tart candies. All in cool colors to reflect her disco theme. Each guest received a black drinking glass with their name on it in gold writing and filled with Jelly Bellies candies in all flavors and colors.

"Wow, what is her wedding going to look like?" Daisy asked me in awe.

"I know! This *is* one fancy party!"

"Well, it is our first event in the new banquet room right Nikki?" Roxy commented.

"For sure." I replied

Everything was almost set, the DJ was playing some music, "Boogie Nights" By Heatwave. The balloon arches in gold were up, and the table cloths in black with gold metallic napkins in the shape of fans in the water glasses were set around the tables.

Matt and Sara arrived first, Sara looked amazing, she frosted her hair and cut it in a butterfly style like Farah Faucet. Matt wore a black suit, no 70s flair for him but he still looked nice.

"Good evening Nikki, you look beautiful," Matt complimented me.

"Thank you, you look pretty nice yourself." This was different he was being nice to me Ok I'd take it.

"Sara, Happy Birthday sweetie you look so pretty."

Sara gave me a pat and an air kiss, we didn't want to mess up our make up right?

"Everything looks perf Nikki!" She clapped with a little jump

"Thank you, Sara."

Sara went and found her reserved table for her and Violet, Jagger, and another friend of theirs, she set her purse down and went to greet her guests that began to arrive.

Matt and I stood by the buffet for a few moments, the silence between us was awkward!

Matt finally broke the silence.

"I heard what happened a couple of days ago, with you and Mrs. Green and Dr. Ferguson."

"Yeah, it was intense, I don't want to experience that again."

I said shaking my head no.

"Mrs. Green told me she is having some trouble dealing with it. How are you doing?" He asked with genuine concern.

"I'm doing fine, there's no permcant damage."

"That's good to hear." He smiled.

"How is everything going with you? Is Sara keeping you on your toes?" I asked him.

"She's great, I like having family around and she ended up doing very well in school this year and in her activities, and she loves her job of course! Things are going well."

Matt and I were making pleasant conversation and it felt good to be friendly again.

"Nikki, I just want to say that..." Matt trailed off as soon as Nick walked into the party and headed our way.

"Nikki, I got your message to meet you here." He smiled giving me a kiss. Now I felt extremely awkward with Matt standing next to me.

"I'm sorry, where are my manners, Nick this is Matt Stevens, he's a friend of mine and Sara's big brother."

"Hi, Nick Williams it's nice to meet you."

"Likewise." Matt replied shaking Nick's hand.

"I'm going to go and get seated." Matt said walking off. Awkward! Ex-boyfriend leaving us, priceless!

"I'm glad you're here Nick, I haven't seen you in a few days, how is everything?"

Nick and I had gone to the beach on Monday, we took our boards and surfed quite a few cool waves. The beach wasn't too crowded so we felt like we had it to ourselves. We had a chance to be just a normal couple. We had an awesome lunch at Dukes, a seafood restaurant and then we walked on the beach later when the sun went down. It was the perfect summer night kind of date with kisses on the beach to the sound of the crashing waves.

I left my daydream of our recent date and tuned into his response.

"I went to see Taylor, he's not doing good! I told him that what he did was unforgivable and that would be the last time that I would see him. I feel terrible for what happened to Kristin and I feel so betrayed by my best friend. The thing is, I'm glad I have you, at least you're the light at the end of the tunnel."

"Well then let's have a great time tonight and enjoy the music and have some fun."

"Sounds great."

We went on the dance floor and mixed it up a little to some great tunes, "Get Down Tonight" By K.C. & The Sunshine Band.

The teens at the party had fun dancing to different disco songs, "Knock on Wood" by Amii Stewart, or "The Groove Line" by Heatwave. The song we opened with was "Celebration" by Kool and The Gang. Everyone loves that song! The room was filled with teens from 15-18 years old and dressed in bellbottoms, halter half tops, maxi dresses, silk pants suits, and even about ten white leisure suits with black dress shirts, a lot of the guys opted for the cliche' Saturday Night Fever suit worn by John Travolta in the movie.

Nick and I danced to a few songs fast and some slow ones. When dinner time arrived all of the guests sat down at their tables and I opened the mic wishing Sara a very happy 16th birthday.

Sara stood and said a few words herself.

"I just wanna thank all of you guys for coming tonight, and sharing my sweet 16th with me, ok let's eat." Everyone clapped.

Nick and I sat at a table with Martin and Oliver and Matt, we were the adult chaperones in the room this evening.

We made small talk, but no one wanted to bring up the arrest of Taylor or the police work that we put in so we talked about the big BBQ coming up at the end of the summer.

"Nikki, have you bought your tickets yet for the annual police BBQ at the end of the summer?" Oliver asked.

"Not yet, I've been busy, I'll get them soon I have two months before the event."

"Well I hear it's going to be the best yet, and guys don't forget the fair is coming to town, oh my it's going to be cowboy nation in Rancho Niguel I better get my spurs."

We all laughed, Oliver enjoyed making jokes and tonight he was lit! Now that dinner was over, the guests were getting back on the dance floor, Martin asked me to dance and so we went onto the dance floor. We danced to a few songs, "Can't get enough of Your Love Baby" By

Barry White and "Ladies Night" By Kool and The Gang. When we went back to our table and left the dance floor we were laughing at some memories Martin had reminded me of. At the table though it seemed like the fun had ended.

Nick had a look of anger on his face, he stood up and whispered in my ear to speak to me privately.

We walked out of the banquet room into the hallway, away from other ears. When we were alone he turned to me.

"Nikki, tell me that what Oliver and Matt told me isn't true?"

"What are you talking about?" I said not having a freaking clue what he meant.

"*You* were the one who found the key pendant in *my* car, and then you thought *I* was the one who killed Kristin! How could you believe that, I thought you trusted me." He took a step back now putting distance between us.

"I'm feeling a little betrayed here, next you're going to tell me you were the one in my house the night someone tried to steal my car!"

I didn't say anything I just looked away.

"Oh my God, I'm right aren't I?" He said feeling the blow of the truth coming to light. The scenario and the fact that I was in his house spying on him did not sit well with him. In my defense, I spoke up and gave my side of the story.

215

"Nick, it *was* a shock when I found the pendant and I did go to the police but by that point, I knew it was Taylor, and I was trying to clear you of any wrongdoing. As far as being in your house, I'm sorry I was searching for clues to find the killer, I didn't know yet what part , if any you had in this. I didn't mean to invade your space or privacy, I guess I just got in over my head!"

He paced a few times absorbing the hit of it, what I told him and now tossing it about in his head to come to a decision.

"I can understand that you were trying to find Kristin's killer but you violated my trust. You found the key pendent in my car and you broke into my house and you didn't even come clean to me after Taylor was arrested, I had to hear it from your friends or should I say a friend and your other ex!" A confused look upon his handsome face.

"I mean do you guys still hang out? You didn't tell me you and Matt were a couple for over two years. He also seems to be around a lot, same with Paul, is this what you do, string guys along so they can follow you like a desperate puppy."

Oh boy, that was low!

"Nick, you don't know the whole story, that's not the way it is!"
I said making my case.

"You know Nikki, this isn't going to work for me, I thought this would be a great relationship with you but, I don't think we have any trust here. Look I wasn't going to say anything tonight, but I was offered a position at Massachusetts General Hospital as head of surgery in Cardiology.

I wasn't going to take the position because I believed we had a great relationship here, but I've changed my mind. I'm sorry Nikki I can't have a relationship without trust! Good luck with everything." He said walking away now and heading for the exit.

"Nick, wait, can't we fix this?"

He turned around for a moment and gave me a look that said maybe, but then he shook his head no and turned and he walked out of Kendle's and my life. That was the last time I saw Nick Williams III. I walked back into the banquet room and my first thought was to direct all of my anger at Matt and Oliver, but Oliver ran to my side.

"Nikki, I misspoke, It had nothing to do with Matt, he didn't say anything, I was having a conversation with Nick and we just sort of began talking about the case and then it just spiraled.

I'm so sorry I saw Nick leave, I can call him and apologize!" Oliver pleaded with me.

We were sitting at the table now with Martin, and then Matt came back to the table after a dance with Sara, she was standing next to him.

"Oliver it's ok, Nick took a job in Massachusetts, he was going to break up with me anyway, so don't worry about it."

I explained with some sadness.

Everyone looked surprised and didn't say anything to me I had looks of concern and empathy from the four of them.

Dumped again, what is wrong with me? Am I going to drive every man away? I thought sulking with sadness.

The silence was deafening until Matt asked me "Nikki can I have this dance?"

I looked up to his warm smile, I stood up and took his hand, and he led me to the dance floor and we slow danced together to the song

"More Than A Woman" by The Bee Gees

Good friends again.

Chapter 31

"Leave The Gun,

Take The Cannoli"

I woke up Sunday morning, not knowing what to make of the past week. After Nick broke it off, my friends came to my side to cheer me up. Sara's party was a big success and her friends were over the moon impressed with it. I sang a song at the end of the evening just like I promised her.

She selected "How Deep is Your Love" By The Bee Gees. They were pretty much the cornerstone for disco at the time besides the queen of disco, Donna Summer, which is why they had so many great songs in the 1970s.

The teens loved the music, they all sang when "Dancing Queen" By ABBA came on and loved "Copa Cabana" By Barry Manilow but with a remix to it that the DJ spiced up.

I even had a few kids ask me if they could rent the place for homecoming next Fall.

Sara thanked me profusely and applauded Chef Stark for the best spread she's ever seen. After the food was gone, the DJ left and the place was cleaned, I left with Chef, a few busboys, and servers and went home.

It was about 9:30 am and I had finished getting ready in lounging shorts and a t-shirt when my doorbell rang. I looked through the ring cam and Roxy waved, she had a box of doughnuts with her.

I opened the door and waved her in. "How did you know I needed a doughnut?"

"Girl, I have something to tell you, have you seen the news this morning?"

"No, why?"

She put the box of doughnuts down on the table and went for my remote control. She turned on the TV and selected the local news station.

The story of the morning was about Dr. Taylor Ferguson.

"We are still here on the scene at the county jail where the warden will have a press conference about the death of Dr. Taylor Ferguson. He was found dead in his cell early this morning by a prison guard! It seems that at this time all we know is that he was possibly poisoned."

"What! Who killed him?" I asked Roxy.

"They don't know who did it, all they know is that he died by being poisoned!" Roxy repeated.

My mind went directly to the fact that this was done intentionally.

I knew that Donnie Giacomo wanted Taylor dead! He had been at the arraignment and was stoic and cold the whole time, he had left the courtroom with reporters hounding him and asking for his thoughts on the case.

Roxy looked at me "Do you think what I'm thinking?"

We both had the same expression on our faces, we knew Donnie was behind it, but the proof was something no one had and no one ever would...

The following Tuesday when I went back to work, I chatted up Chef Stark.

"It's crazy what happened to Taylor Ferguson isn't it?" I asked him

"Karma has a way of coming to those who do wrong." This was all chef said. A chill went up and down my spine.

Later that day I was up in my office when Chef Stark came up the staircase. "Nikki there is a friend here to see you."

I walked to my sofas from my office, "Oh who has come to pay me a visit." I smiled.

Donnie Giacomo stood there in a black pinstripe suit.

"Mr. Giacomo it's nice to see you again." He shook my hand.

"Nikki, I can't stay too long but I just had to thank you in person for all of your help with finding my Kristin's killer. I just want you to know if you ever need anything just give me a ring or let Tony know." He pointed to Chef Stark.

"Thank you, I appreciate that."

"Well, I'm also here to say goodbye, I'm moving to Italy, Tuscany to be exact, my family has been asking me to move there for many years. I have cousins and aunts and uncles and finally, I decided this was the best time to move. It's what you call early retirement." He smiled with happiness.

"Wow Tuscany, what a beautiful place, with wonderful food, I'm jealous."

He chuckled.

"You should come for a visit one day,"

"I just might one of these days."

"You get there you look me up and we'll have dinner." He offered.

"I will, thank you, and have a safe trip."

" Thank you." He tipped his fedora hat and left out the private staircase...

The next day I called Mrs. Green to check up on her

"Hi Mrs. Green, I was just calling to see how you are doing and if you would like to be my guest for dinner tomorrow."

"Oh that would be lovely Nikki, of course, I would. Oh did you hear that Donnie moved to Italy?"

"Yes, he came to see me, right before his flight. I'm glad. He's moved on, he seemed happy." I told her

"I guess it was therapeutic for him to visit Dr. Ferguson in prison." She responded.

"Wait, he did what?" I couldn't believe my ears and they were burning to know more! So she continued.

"He went to pay a visit to Dr. Taylor Ferguson, I guess he told him he forgave him because he told me he felt much better. He said it was one of those moments you know leave the gun take the cannoli, or whatever that means, I thought it was an interesting metaphor." She chuckled.

I nearly dropped the phone, Donnie had pretty much admitted responsibility for the death of Dr. Taylor Ferguson, Roxy and I were right.

"Mrs. Green have you ever watched the movie "The Godfather?"
She hesitated for a moment.

"Oh many, many years ago when it first came out, I think I was in college, why do you ask?"

"No reason! Now about dinner tomorrow what time is good for you?"

Epilogue

A high of 92 degrees, and right in the middle of summer, the heat was bringing in the customers. I had to have another ice machine brought in because of the massive amount we were using.

After the whole Nick Williams episode I told Jessica and Roxy in a nice way to stop setting me up on dates. I'm still single and right now it's the best course for me.

As for the trip that Nick and I won, LINKED TO THE HEART sent me the gift certificate for it. I took it and raffled it off at Wednesday's Disco night.

I raised $2000.00 dollars and then I matched it with a donation of $10k and the proceeds I sent to Ella and Janice the nurses that Kristin was close friends with. Mrs. Green told me they started a scholarship in Kristin's name for women in the RN program at the local college.

The Mayor walked in with my good friend Marge today, I had made it clear that Stacie was not allowed in Kendle's after her alcoholic outburst towards me.

The Mayor respected my wishes and didn't let it affect her business friendship with me.

"I have your usual table out on the patio and the misters are on so it should keep you two cool."

When I sat them at their table CJ Groves gave me the good news, "Nikki, we have finished the boardwalk at Lake Santa Arianna, and we are having the ribbon cutting on Monday, oh I can't wait, it will be WONDERFUL!" She clapped her hands.

"I can't wait too, it will be nice to take a dip in the lake, and after all of the construction, I bet a lot of folks are anxious to get in there. I believe you had some lifeguards hired for the beach area of the lake is that correct?"

"Yes, Nikki you won't believe the time Marge had trying to recruit lifeguards in the middle of summer, you know because generally all of these decisions are made months before!

But we have five of them now on the two towers and then we had to hire people for daily maintenance.

Oh, you wouldn't believe how busy we have been."

She carried on describing her troubles, the city demands so much she always said.

"I'll say I'm ready for a cold margarita Nikki, I'll start with that!" Marge replied looking deflated with heat exhaustion.

"Ok, and Ms. Mayor how about you?"

"I'll take a Pina Colada please." She flipped her hair and put her shades back on.

"Coming right up." I told her.

I went to the bar and gave Tito the drink order,

"I'll take these over myself, Nikki." Tito said.

"Hey guess what I heard Lake Santa Arianna is opening next week, get your boat ready."

"I heard boss, the boat is clean and ready for the water. Daisy and I are going on opening day, you should join us?"

"Maybe I will, I need some downtime."

"Now you're talkin' boss!"

I went up to my office and brought up the website for Lake Santa Arianna.

The information boasted about the lake getting a makeover, they added a long boardwalk or a pier-like structure constructed by the beach part of the large lake. They added retail space and snack shacks, and some games like ring toss, fill the balloon with a water gun, and many more. The surrounding park was green and filled with a blanket of orange poppies everywhere, small benches sat in front of the lake for taking a rest. There are walking paths, picnic shelters, and tables.

Two boat launches and a small booth for boat rentals, It looked fabulous, I couldn't wait!

Just then my phone range to the tune of "Kokomo" from The Beach Boys

"Hello Roxy"

"Hey, Nikki I have a request for you girly."

"Ok, shoot!"

"I need your help on a petition to save the Rancho Arianna historic home, I can't believe someone wants to purchase it and the land it's on, only to demolish it, to build condos around the lake, we can't have this, Nikki you have to help me. I've started to collect signatures on a petition and I contacted some organizations that specialize in community preservation!"

"Count me in Roxy, you know I'm all about preservation, let's get a game plan together."

"Ok, girl it's on!"

Don't miss the next Nikki Rodriguez Adventure

Boardwalk, Blackmail and Beach Music

It's the middle of summer, so get your bathing suit and beach towel. Everyone in Rancho Niguel has gone to Lake Santa Arianna to lie in the sun on the sandy beach, and cruise by on their motor boats. The temperature at the lake is cool and brisk when Matt and Nikki discover the body of Hawk McGuire stabbed under the boardwalk! A greedy real estate mogul that was set to tear down a historic mansion! Soon Roxy becomes the number one suspect as the leader of the community group fighting for the preservation of the Rancho Arianna Mansion and Estate. Paul and Craig have their hands full patrolling the lake for clues to solve the case and Stacie strikes again in her wrath to get Paul back and destroy Nikki. Will everyone have a bitch n' summer or will a killer drive off into the sunset?

Here is a sample of

Boardwalk, Blackmail

And Beach Music

Prologue

The summer sun shined bright over the crowd of people standing with solidarity at the sight of the grand dam herself, the Rancho Arianna Mansion and Estate. Currently held as a museum with lush gardens. Roxy Carmichael president of The Arts and Preservation Society, spoke clearly and concisely at the podium in front of the boat dock by the lake.

"We must preserve this estate for the future of our community we owe it to past generations to continue to carry on in support of our historical buildings." Nikki sat in a chair to the left of the podium quietly listening to Roxy's speech.

The large crowd had doubled in size this afternoon since word of the protest had circulated the city, many came from other cities as well to show support for the historical preservation society - Rancho Niguel chapter, that partnered up with The Arts and Preservation Society.

"We must stop the vicious greed perpetrating our communities in an effort to demolish our founding homes and lands that built our communities. Don't we have enough condos? Don't we have enough mini-malls? The historical society and I have come up with some wonderful options to bring in funding for the upkeep of the estate built in 1903. We have put our ideas together and have come up with turning this 20-acre estate into a non for profit fabulous lodge or Inn, with room for events and galas, a fine art gallery, a spa, and 50 guest rooms for affordable vacation rental fees all year-long overlooking the lake. As for this boat launch, we look forward to turning it into a full-time marina, renting out boat slips for moorage, and keeping prices at record-low levels for all of the community to afford. The current boat house will also rent out boats, canoes, kayaks, and windboards. On the grounds, we will also add some small cottages lakefront for vacation rental. The cost has come to $5 million dollars to upgrade and renovate the estate, with a grant obtained by the county for more than half of that amount. We have private donations that have come in for 1.5 million dollars, so now we have to raise $500,000 dollars. All of the funds from the inn and boat rentals will go to provide estate upkeep and staff payroll, security services, and a public park. So what do you say, ladies and gentlemen, we can do it!"

Later that night when everyone had left the lake for the evening, a man drove up to the mansion and parked his

Porsche in the circular driveway. He opened his car door and walked to the front of the mansion entryway. Large with a lush green lawn and a vast garden, the man stood to the side of the huge concrete fountain with a mural of mermaids engraved in green stone. The fountain low but in front of the estate made for a grand entrance. Another lone figure walked toward the man, the figure handed the man an envelope the size of a letter. "Here is the report on the stability of this dump, it needs about $5 million in renovations and they don't have the money to cover it. The city wants it sold and fast before the protesters are really heard."

The man looked over the contents of the envelope! "So it's a done deal I can purchase the estate and then demolish it for my 300-plus condo community?"

"Sure, but we have to get it through the city council vote, the Mayor will do whatever they say."

"That's no problem I have secured at least one member that will encourage the other members of the council to vote my way."

The man smiled in spite of his nefarious business dealings.

"Whatever, do you have my money?" The stranger asked.

"Here." The man handed off a white handle bag filled with $100s in four stacks.

The stranger took out a counterfeit pen, "It's not that I don't trust you but I don't trust you."

"It's real and all there." The man said, sarcasm dripping from his words.

The stranger finished up and put the money back in the bag.

"Ok, I'll be in touch."

The man got back in his Porsche and the stranger walked off.

The man turned on his car and drove away laughing to himself,

"By next week I'll have made myself richer than I ever imagined."

Chapter 1

Boats, Boats, Boats

The grand opening this morning was spectacular, Little Black Dress among three other bands performed on the new boardwalk on Lake Santa Arianna. We kicked off to the tune of "Soak up the Sun" By Sheryl Crow.

With the lake under us, shimmering in the sunshine, boats drifted in the distance and people made their way strolling the boardwalk to the end of the pier where we had the stage. Snack stands and retail booths were in full motion, servicing many customers. Kids with their parents, strolled with balloons in yellow, white, and emerald green, holding large swirls of pink cotton candy.

The smell of hot dogs grilled and burgers sizzling wafted through the air. My stomach growled just from the thought of food at this time. Breakfast this morning had been skimpy just coffee and a bagel with cream cheese and now I was more than ready for lunch.

The band played two more songs, "Is This Love" by Bob Marley and "Hot Fun in the Summertime" By Sly and The Family Stone.

This song makes you just want to take a stroll on the boardwalk, I sang the song as a duet with Tito, with the girls playing the background music and vocals. We wrapped it up to a cheering audience. After stepping down from the stage, the band met up at The Burger Shack. We sat down at a table on the patio. Cheeseburgers all around and ice teas.

"I love singing with you gals."

Tito said taking a drink of his Iced tea.

"We've been doing some great duet songs, why didn't we think of this before." I replied.

"Hey, Tito did you bring your boat?" Roxy asked.

"I sure did, Daisy and I dropped it off in a slip an hour and a half ago, she's meeting me back here in about 20 minutes. She had to go and get some snacks and drinks. You guys all up for skirting around the lake?" He asked us.

"Not for us Tito we have a baseball game with our company." Dana and Taylor my band members replied.

"I've got a baby shower for my sister-in-law later today guys, rain check?" Emily my other guitarist asked.

"Sure we have all summer it's only early August, this is California we can boat well into November." Tito smiled his pearly whites gleaming.

"August 1, to be exact so that means we have like 90 days or something right?" Roxy asked.

The new band on stage began with "Don't Worry Baby"

By The Beach Boys.

We sang along to the song briefly, "I love this song." I said.

"Ladies and Tito, congratulations on a fabulous job I caught the show here." Matt came up behind our table walking into the patio dressed in a pair of blue Hawaiian print board shorts and a light grey t-shirt, and slip-on white Vans.

"Thanks," I replied.

"Have a seat." Roxy told Matt.

He sat down across from me next to Tito, he looked like he had been out on the lake already, his tan a shade darker.

"So what's new Matt?" Roxy asked him.

"I bought a new boat." He smiled.

"What no way, the Bayliner you were looking at, congrats man!"

Tito bro'd a high five with Matt.

"Yeah, I just got the keys a few days ago, I have her in the lake at the boat house right now, you guys want to go for a ride?"

I shot a look at Tito I was going out with Daisy and him in a few minutes, but before I spoke up, Roxy intercepted.

"Matt I promised I would go out with Tito and Daisy but Nikki can go with you."

Tito pipped in "Yeah Nikki, we'll catch you later."

Matt smiled and turned to me "How about it?"

I had been blindsided by my bestie, and now Tito! Once again Cupid's apprentice Roxy the heart maker set me up. I thought of calling her Madam Roxy maybe that was more fitting for her, I didn't have time to shoot her a look of "Oh no lady stop setting me up" but it was too late Matt was staring at me with those amazing baby blues patiently waiting for an answer.

"Yeah, that sounds like fun, I just need to change." I pointed to my L.L. Bean boat tote in red and canvas beige.

"The boat house has a changing cabana." Matt offered.

I had no way out of this one, so I agreed with a smile. "Sure that would be fine."

We all got up from the table and made our way out, I said bye to the gals in my band and away from Matt's eyes, I shot Roxy a look that said we'll talk later girlfriend!

She laughed and said, "Have fun you two!"

Tito just smiled and gave me the thumbs-up signal.

I had changed in the boat house cabana, a small room with a bathroom and a mirrored vanity.

Today I sported a tankini bathing suit from Tommy Bahama, it's so cute the color is a beautiful vibrant blue and white in a hibiscus floral print. A halter spaghetti strap and the bottoms are the same color and pattern. I saw it last week and grabbed one. I added a white long sleeve seer sucker button-down shirt over my suit.

I put my clothes in my bag and put on my white slip-on Keds, better to have anti-slip footing on a boat right?

I walked down to the slip where Matt's boat sat slowly moving with the current of the lake. Anchored at this time and steady enough for me to ease on into the back of the boat, Matt held my hand to help me in. It was very nice, the outside of the boat was two-tone white on the top and dark blue on the lower part. The seats were white too with dark blue trim.

DX2250 is what it said in small stainless steel lettering under the large cursive writing that read *Bayliner* on the side of the boat.

The boat was spotless and new, everything was shiny and polished. The seats had the words BAYLINER on the top part of the seating area on the back of the boat. A small walkway led to the area where you could jump off the boat into the water. Along with a sunbathing deck off the back of the boat too.

The Bow had more seating resembling a circular seating area past the driver and passenger seats. It was like a sunk-in nook. Very cool!

I stowed my bag in a compartment under one of the bench seats and put my cell in a compartment by the steering wheel that Matt told me was waterproof.

"Find a seat and we'll head out. He had on a pair of dark Oakley sunglasses, I selected the seat across from his and put on my shades. I had put my hair in a low ponytail to keep it from flying all over the place. One thing about these boats, they were hell on hair.

He started the engine and off we went, gliding into the blue water in the blazing sun. We sped around the large lake a few times going by other boats and passing the large Rancho Arianna Mansion and Estate. Matt turned on the speakers and put music on via his blue tooth on his phone. We pulled into a nice little spot on the other side of the lake with views of the hills. He turned off the engine and we anchored for lunch. He pulled out some drinks from a small fridge under the small sink in the middle of the boat. He handed me a Coke and asked me to put the small portable table on the back seats. I went ahead and placed it in the holes on the bottom of the seats and we had a table for our lunch. The song "Boat Ride" By Brian Kelley played on the speakers. Matt brought out two plastic blue plates with cold fried chicken, potato salad, and a bowl of cold strawberries. His boat had a retractable canopy above, giving us some much-needed shade!

"You did good Captain Stevens, this is exactly what I wanted for lunch."

He smiled back at me and then took a bite of his chicken, I know it's one of your favorites."

"Yours too buddy, and the country music, this is totally you!" I chuckled.

"Don't knock the country, you know I'm just a cowboy at heart." He laughed.

We had some small talk about current events in the city and his team at the firehouse, the band, Kendle's, and my new Jeep. The music went from "Summer Time" to "Guitars and Tiki Bars" by Kenny Chesney.

"So tell me the truth how are you really?"

I knew he was wondering if I was still upset about Nick Williams dumping me at Sara's party last month. I was over him, truthfully, but I felt like being dumped was normal for me.

"I'm over it all, really. It's a good thing he left, he was more committed to his career and I don't think it would have worked in the long run anyway."

"I didn't see you as a doctor's wife honestly." Matt replied.

"I know it scares you." He replied.

I wasn't sure what he meant by that comment, should I be offended or complemented?

"I'm going to be honest, someday yes of course I'd like to get married and have kids, the house, and the family pets but I'm doing it on my terms." I told him.

"I wouldn't expect anything less, you are very independent, and that scares some guys."

"Does that include you too?"

"I'll be honest, no! Nick was a fool! He didn't understand who you were and what he had!

I admit I had been a fool too! I was upset about the whole Sara issue, and it took me four months to see why you did what you did and even though I don't agree with you keeping it from me I understand why you did."

"So you're still not over it?"

"I'm over it! I realized that if you had to lie to me to protect someone in my family that I love very much, then that sacrifice is honorable. I'm not going to be a fool again Nikki Rodriguez, I want you back."

Chapter 2

Under The Boardwalk, Oh No!

After our late lunch, we took the boat around one more time gliding

through the blue water of the lake and relaxing to the tunes of beachy/

island music. "Margarita Ville" by Jimmy Buffet played and then "Stir

it up" by Bob Marley. We swam in cool blue water for a while and I

sunbathed on that lovely deck. I thought about what Matt said, he

wanted to get back together.

I told him it was a little soon from my last relationship but that we

should be friends and continue to let it naturally evolve. I also told him

I still had feelings for Paul and until that was resolved I wasn't making

any relationship official. He agreed and told me that was fair and that

he wanted our relationship built on trust and full commitment. Yeah,

that word was scary but he didn't push and we decided to just move

along slowly. After one more go around the lake, we then decided to

call it a day.

I was glad that I had put on sunblock and now my tan became more

Hawaiian tropical island girl. It was around 5:30 pm and even though the lake was still filled with boaters and jet skiers and the sun was still high, we were tired.

I opened my beach bag and pulled on a pair of denim shorts and tied my shirt at the waist. Matt docked the boat in one of the boat slips and we made our way towards the boardwalk. Matt volunteered to drive me home since I didn't have my car here. I told him I had to make one stop first. I had to go to the city sub-office located at the end of the boardwalk by the restaurant called The Lake House.

"I'll just be a minute, I need to pick up the check for the band from Emma the city office manager."

"Ok, I'll wait here." Matt stood outside the small office building, leaning on a lamp post checking his phone. I walked into the small office and spotted Emma. She was getting ready to lock up, her pale pink summer dress still looked fabulous the crisp linen without a wrinkle. "Nikki, I'm so glad you're here, I was going to just mail your check off, but now that you're here, well here you go." She handed me a white envelope with the city logo, a mountain in blue with the sun in yellow setting down. I had come to know these envelopes very well, having a city check cut for the band over the last six years or so.

"Thank you, Emma, if you have any other events you need us for just give me a ring." I told her heading for the door.

"Nikki, I did want to ask you a question."

"What is it, Emma?" I asked.

"I was wondering are you still friends with Detective Anderson?"

This caught me a little off guard why would Emma want to know this? I had only interacted with her professionally as a city employee, never discussing anything private or for a social talk.

"Yes, we are friends still." I smiled politely.

"I know this may sound strange since we are business acquaintances but I'm worried about Detective Anderson."

"Why? What's going on?"

"It has to do with Stacie."

I was intrigued with my ears on full-blown high-frequency.

"Please go on." I said.

"Marge and I are good friends and we were talking about Stacie one day and we came to the conclusion that she has some ulterior motives for her job and for Detective Anderson and so Marge confided in me about what she thinks Stacie is after and so I've been watching her as well and yesterday I noticed that she and the mayor went to her house and they didn't return for several hours. Then when Mayor CJ returned she looked like a ghost, her eyes were clear but she wasn't there, she looked like she was in a trance or something. When I tried to speak with her Stacie cut between us and said that Mayor CJ was suffering from a migraine and she took some medication. I told Marge it was so strange, it didn't seem like Mayor CJ knew what was happening to her."

"What kind of medication did she take?"

"Stacie said it was aspirin." Emma said looking like it was a strange thing.

"Aspirin wouldn't have that kind of reaction, for her." I responded.

"Nikki, then when she went to lunch with Detective Anderson on another day he had that same look on his face, and Stacie said he was just tired from solving the case last week about the murder of Kristin Cabela and saving Nikki's Hyde once again. She said it in a very menacing way too!"

"Emma, let me look into this and I'll be in touch ok."

"Thanks, Nikki, I just feel like there's something not right."

I walked out of the office, Matt and I walked slowly as of course my mind was spinning with questions and thoughts.

What was Stacie up to?

I reached into my bag and took out my cashmere wrap and draped it around my shoulders, the chill in the air suddenly came on.

We reached the end of the pier/boardwalk and Matt broke the silence.

"I was wondering if you were still here, you seemed distracted."

"Oh, sorry, it's nothing I'm just tired, a little too much sun I guess." I said nonchalantly dismissing it.

I walked on and went down the side ramp from the pier to the edge of the lake. Matt followed me.

I stood on the sand looking at the blue calm thinking about what Emma told me.

"Nikki, are you ready to go?" Matt asked as he stood beside me.

Just then the wind picked up and my wrap that I had around my shoulders went flying away, Matt and I went under the pier to get it.

"That's my favorite wrap it's silk and cashmere." I said running to get it. Matt stopped for an instant, "Nikki, I think you might need to replace it.

When I caught up to him my white wrap lay on top of a body in the bloody sand under the boardwalk!

"Oh no!" I said out loud!

Chapter 3

Murder On The Beach

Paul and Craig were the detectives on the scene this evening, Sonya another police detective, and my friend was on vacation in Mexico with her husband so it was just the boys on the case.

Craig was interviewing Matt, and Paul came over to speak with me.

"Nikki, are you ok?" He put his hand on my shoulder.

"Just a little shaken right now." I replied.

"Take a deep breath, let it go and just take your time. Just start from the beginning and tell me what happened?" His green eyes filled with concern.

I gave him the run down from the time Matt and I left the city hub office on the boardwalk, to the wind coming and taking my wrap and when we followed to retrieve it. We found him! He wrote down every detail not missing a beat.

"Ok, it looks like I have all of the information I need right now, I'll give you a call if I need anything else." Paul said closing his small notebook and walking away to get one last detail from the coroner.

I thought about the body lying there in the sand under the boardwalk, how long had he been there? The coroner had packed up the body and drove the van off to the morgue to do the autopsy. I went over the whole thing again in my mind making sure I gave every detail to Paul I could possibly remember. A few minutes later I walked over to Craig, Matt and now Paul joined us.

"Any idea who this guy was? How long has he been dead?" I asked.

"He's been dead about two hours, and the body belongs to Hawkins McGuire, better known as the Hawk, real estate tycoon." Craig responded.

"The man that wants to tear down the Rancho Arianna mansion! Oh my gosh!" I raked my hand through my hair in disbelief.

"Bingo!" Craig replied punctuating this with his finger in the air.

"No way!" Matt called out astonished rubbing his jaw.

"Yeah, the big mogul that has been havoc on SoCal." Paul chimed in. The reputation of Hawk the real estate mogul was that he tore down old historical homes and buildings and made way for shiny and new commercial or residential buildings all crammed together with minimal architecture and cheap materials.

"Who would kill him though?" I asked.

Paul and Craig looked at one another

"We do have a possible suspect." Paul said quietly.

"Who?" Matt and I said in unison.

"Roxy." Paul said with a look of concern.

"What! How or why?" I asked in disbelief.

"The murder weapon was found under the body, he was stabbed with a drumstick!" Craig told us.

"That's ridiculous Roxy would never. She would never hurt anyone let alone use one of her drumsticks. I don't believe it!" I clamored.

"Roxy wouldn't do this." Matt called out shaking his head no!

"We have to follow the evidence, Nikki, I don't make the rules." Paul responded with a glare.

He walked off to talk to a fellow officer in blues.

"I gotta get going Nikki, I don't think Roxy did it either." Craig said then he headed off to the other officers clustered around the crime scene.

"You ready to go home, Nikki?"

"Yes."

I walked to Matt's red truck in a daze replaying the conversation that just took place.

Matt drove to the boat launch and retrieved his boat, hooked it up to the trailer hitch on the back of his truck, and locked it in place.

I got in the truck and we drove off. Soft music played from his XM radio, "Little Surfer Girl"

by The Beach Boys.

When we got to my place I thanked Matt for a cool day

on the lake but that I had to talk to Roxy and fast.

He understood and told me if I needed anything to call him and tell Roxy that he's on her side.

"Thanks, Matt, see ya later." I grabbed my bag and went into my condo.

I dialed Roxy's number and told her what happened.

"Roxy I'm calling my stepdad Jeff's lawyer don't say a word to Paul or Craig just tell them you will need to speak with legal counsel."

"Well Nikki, you might want to hurry, they just showed up."

"Don't say a word!"

"Ok."

Chapter 4

Attorney Please

After I hung up with Roxy I dialed the family attorneys at the Wexler, Hyatt, Johnson, and Newman firm.

The office said they would send their top criminal attorney out right away, so I gave them Roxy's address.

I quickly changed into a pair of black pants and a black and white silk sleeveless blouse. I put on some Micheal Kor's black low-heeled sandals and grabbed my keys and drove over to Roxy's place.

Paul and Craig's police car Charger was parked outside of Roxy's apartment. She lived in a four-plex off of Main Street, next to the movie theatre.

I knocked on the door and Roxy let me in, I hugged her and went in. Roxy's platinum blond do was set in a low bun with her usual red chopsticks crosswise in her hair.

She was dressed in an A-line sleeveless dress in a floral print.

Paul and Craig were having a glass of water, at the kitchen table.

"Did you say anything?" I whispered to Roxy

"No, they just got here."

I walked over to Detective Anderson and Detective Zane

"Nikki, what are you doing here?" Paul asked not happy to see me

"Roxy is waiting for legal counsel, the lawyer should be here soon."

Paul stood up "We just need to ask Roxy a few questions it's routine that's it."

"Then you won't mind if she has a lawyer." I replied.

I sat down and smiled "Craig how is Kiana doing?"

"Great Nikki, thanks for asking." He smiled.

Paul gave him a glare, Craig sat up straiter and then began with

"Nikki maybe we should just get this over with, We're not arresting Roxy, just questioning her."

The doorbell rang and Roxy ran to answer it.

Roxy came back with a tall gal in a blue suit. Her flawless makeup on her coco skin was smooth without a wrinkle.

"I'm Deidre Johnson, legal counsel for Ms. Carmichael!" She put her hand out to Paul and Craig.

"Detective Anderson and this is Detective Zane, let's get started." He said point blank but with a brash of redness at the end of his sentence.

"Detective, I've been briefed on the evidence you have and there are no fingerprints, no records of my client having any connection to the murder weapon.

Plus she has an alibi. After being on stage for two hours she was on the boat all afternoon with friends and then went to dinner with the same group of friends and I have witnesses willing to testify to it. This meeting is over fellas!"

Wow, this woman kicked butt! She left Craig with his mouth open gaping at the marvel of Miss Deidra's control of the conversation.

Paul stood up, not happy with the conversation but he knew she was right.

"We have letters that were written to the victim from Roxy and there is the motive to remove Mr. McGuire so that he wouldn't be in her way to purchase and demolish the Rancho Arianna Mansion." He told her.

"All of the letters were written in a business and professional manner, with CC copies sent to the Mayor herself. As for motive you have no evidence of that and all of it is speculation."

Paul and Craig made their way to the door, Craig left his business contact card with Deidra and they walked out to their car.

After Craig and Paul left Deidra sat down and went over what they had.

"Ladies they have nothing, and I am aware that you had a dislike for the victim but that is all and if everyone who disliked someone was arrested everyone would be in jail.

If they want to speak with you tell them you will only do so with me there."

"Wow, you were amazing, you must be the best lawyer I've ever met." Roxy told her.

"She was top of her class at Stanford, and Miss Deidra just became the youngest female to make partner at her firm, you know Jeff only hires the best."

"Oh thank you Nikki." Deidra smiled

"Here is my private line if you need me in a hurry." She handed Roxy her business card.

"Thanks," Roxy replied.

After Deidra left Roxy and I had a glass of wine.

"So now this is put on my shoulders because I led the group against this guy's business." Roxy remarked.

"Look you didn't do this and I doubt anyone from the Rancho Historical Society or The Arts and Preservation Society would do anything like this."

"The thing is we need to find out who would!"

Chapter 5

Rancho Santa Arianna

A few days later when the news of the murder of Hawk McGuire, Real Estate mogul died down a bit (no pun intended) the Historical Society and The Arts and Preservation Society at Rancho Niguel, met at the grand mansion. Roxy our president, our Executive Assistant Rhonda Timbers, and I the VP, were invited to the meeting with the city council and the mayor. Also in attendance was Dr. Neal Forbes from the Historical Society. The four of us sat in the main hall, a room that was used for parties and large dinners, now it was used as an auditorium for the museum. White wooden chairs sat in rows of six facing the front wall of the room.

Large windows adorned the opposite side of the room allowing for plenty of sunlight that brought warmth. We arrived early and took our seats in the second row. A podium was placed on a six-foot table up front with chairs for the members of the city council and the Mayor.

"The council is set to vote today on the future of the estate but do you think they will postpone it due to the recent events, in regard to Mr. McGuire?"

Dr. Neal Forbes asked us to make conversation, while we waited.

"I was told that there would be a vote." Roxy replied

The members of the board arrived along with the Mayor, and a few representatives from Hawk McGuire's real estate firm.

"They must have carpooled together." I whispered to Roxy.

"I would be surprised they could all fit into one car with the egos on that group." We chuckled.

The mayor sat down at her seat up front by the podium, her evil Gidget hair flip now in light caramel, went lovely with her yellow floral top and white slacks. She was a stylish and smart dresser I'd give her that.

Stacie sat down behind our row but at the end of it so she was four seats away from us. She had a large notebook with her, a low-cut lavender blouse, and a smug look on her face.

Roxy and I looked at one another, wondering what was next.

"We would like to bring this meeting to order now!"

The mayor sounded off.

The four of us sat up poised and prepared for the vote to come.

"I would like to thank everyone for coming today in spite of the tragedy that has taken place right under our great new boardwalk, what a terrible thing to happen."

She looked down now playing up the humanitarian concern.

Yeah right!

"I have spoken with the board and we have decided..."

She stopped for just a second as Craig and Paul took a seat in our row on the last two seats. I looked at Paul and smiled, he smiled back but then looked forward.

The mayor continued her speech for us. " We have decided to postpone the vote!"

"What? That's not fair!" Roxy yelled out.

I shook my head at her telling her not to say another word!

Craig and Paul looked at Roxy, I stood up right away and said:

"Thank you, Ms. Mayor we understand that at this time that would be the best thing to do."

She acknowledged me with "Nikki, I knew you would understand, and folks we will still take your ideas and let you be heard up front at the podium. We are a civilized democracy you know." She gave a look of intent to her words. "Dr. Neal Forbes, you are up first."

Evil Gidget smiled and then sat down.

I had a chance to scan the room and it seemed we had more people from the community here now, a few of them held signs that read; SAVE RANCHO ARIANNA in red writing on white poster boards. Dr. Forbes went to the podium and began his speech for the pro-save the estate side of the vote. We clapped for him and the protesters cheered him on. Roxy sulked in her chair, arms crossed over her chest and her full red lips in a pout!

I had to keep her from incriminating herself especially with Paul and Craig sitting a few seats from us.

Stacie got up from her seat and tried to squeeze into the empty seat where Dr. Forbes was sitting between Paul and Rhonda. I was next to Rhonda on her left, and of course, Dr. Forbes would be back after his speech. Who the heck did she think she was?

Rhonda had her purse sitting on the empty seat when Stacie told her: "Can you move your purse?" She whispered but stood with her foot tapping. I knew she just wanted to sit next to Paul. I could see the look on Craig's face he just raised his eyebrows no doubt he was aware of Stacy's methods.

Rhonda the sweet gal she was, and a little reluctant, replied "Dr. Forbes will be coming back to his seat."

Stacie pushed Rhonda's purse to the floor, she sat down right away, with a look of satisfaction on her face.

Paul whispered to her "Was that necessary? You're being rude."

Poor Rhonda just picked up her purse but had a look of being slapped, her face was flushed pink and red. At that point, something inside me erupted!

I stood up and yelled, "You owe her an apology, Stacie!"

Dr. Forbes, stopped his speech and the room went silent!

"Oh yeah, who's going to make me?" She stood up.

Rhonda slid over to my seat and I was face to face with Stacie.

"I am!" I told her, our eyes locked on one another. Craig and Paul got up now "Ladies let's all sit down and be calm." Craig quietly suggested.

"Shut up Craig!" Stacie spat out!

"Someone needs to teach you some manners." I told her.

Paul's arm was on her pulling her back.

"Back off Paul, I can handle this!" Stacie smirked and when her open hand made contact with my face, I returned with a fist. She fell back into Paul and touched her cheek,

"My face!" She cried out!

Paul pulled her out of the aisle and they walked off. Craig grabbed me and walked me out of the room. The commotion now had an audience that was focused on us, Dr. Forbes was still silent and the peaceful protesters didn't utter a word, only holding up their cell phones no doubt recording the incident.

When we got outside Paul was lecturing Stacie on the front steps.

Craig let my arm go and then he said.

"Good left hook Nikki, that broad get's on my nerves."

"She was so rude to everyone and I guess I just blew, I'm sorry Craig I don't believe violence is the way to go."

"You're good Nikki, she hit first, just walk it off." I rubbed the side of my face, being slapped by someone with rings on was not cool. I could see Stacie's face swelling and some bruising coming to her cheek. Paul was really laying into her, the veins in his neck actually popped out. I had never seen him that upset, he was always so calm and cool.

He walked to Craig and me. Stacie stayed planted where she was.

"Nikki!"

"I'm sorry Paul I shouldn't have hit her, but she hit me first." I calmly pointed out.

He didn't say anything more except "Are you ok?"

"I'll be fine."

By now many people had come outside to witness the commotion. The Mayor ran over to us, "Ladies please let's be civilized, no fighting, we can resolve our disputes peacefully, there's no reason for violence now." She said with a plastic smile.

"Everything is fine Ms. Mayor, there is no need to worry, we have diffused the situation." Craig told her.

"Oh good, ok well we adjured the meeting so I guess we will reconvene later next week. Stacie I need to speak with you." The mayor called out now heading toward Stacie.

Roxy, Dr. Forbes, and Rhonda came up to me now.

"Thank you Nikki for standing up for me." Rhonda quietly said, she had her purse on her shoulder and calmly left to her car.

Dr. Forbes shook my hand and bid Roxy and me farewell he would be at the next meeting. Roxy pulled me inside the building and we went back to the museum side of the mansion. The rooms downstairs displayed artwork, sculptures, and paintings. We went to a parlor room off the dining area, a set of two-person teak benches sat in the middle of the pale peach room.

"Nikki, I'm so glad you stood up to her, I couldn't believe how she bullied poor Rhonda."

"Roxy I just broke, she was so mean I just had to say something."

"Yeah and did you see that smirk on her face when she took the seat? Man, she's really something and then telling Craig to shut up, you should have seen the look on his face, I thought he was going to haul her out and beat her! Does your face hurt?" She asked scrunching her face.

"I'm good don't worry."

We took a tour of the place, the rooms upstairs were about forty of them, and it was as large as a small hotel. We only saw about maybe ten rooms, Roxy had ideas for making each one a slight nautical theme. "One hundred and twenty years old, It's so classic, the built-in alcoves, bookshelves, and even the built-in buffets and hutches. You don't see 1903 architecture like this anymore, with custom crown molding and stained glass windows. This style is a cross between Mediterranean and turn-of-the-century style. Look at these sinks, so timeless, and all of the door nobs are lead crystal. It's beautiful!" I told Roxy

"The furniture is dated circa 1901, can you imagine destroying it, I can't." Roxy replied.

The backstory of the Rancho Santa Ariana Mansion was a romantic one. The mansion was built by Aiden Packard for his wife Arianna Niguel. The story goes that she was a wealthy socialite born to a family that owned all of Rancho Niguel or formally the town called Haven Valley. They farmed citrus, oranges, limes, lemons, grapefruit, and tangerines. They also owned the third-largest winery in the state. Arianna, at 18 fell in love with Aiden Packard, a poor 23-year-old iron worker from Los Angeles. The family feeling that he didn't measure up forbade the reunion and sent poor Arianna away to San Fransisco to attend college. After six years of being away from home, Arianna finally came back to Haven Valley. When she arrived she found out that Aiden and his family had struck oil in their backyard and became the fourth wealthiest family in the west. Aiden went to college and earned a business degree and became the president of Packard Oil, his family business. He also had a fiancé and was scheduled to be married in a few days. Upon hearing this Arianna went to see Aiden and after one day together, they declared their undying love for one another and eloped the next day. The scandal was hard for her family and they disowned her. Aiden and Arianna were happy they had three children and Aiden commissioned the home to be built on the lake calling it Rancho Santa Arianna. Eventually, her family came around and on his deathbed, her father left her the winery and the 1000 acres of orchards.

They happily lived at Ranch Santa Arianna for the next 15 years until Aiden was killed in a car crash in 1918. Arianna stayed in the home until her death in 1958 and she never remarried. Her children were given their inheritance, with the wishes that the orchards be donated to the city. In 1961 the city changed its name to Rancho Niguel. The Vineyard was eventually sold by the family and the home was later sold in 1982 to the city. Arianna and Aidens children have long passed and she had two grandsons and four great-grandkids left. The family sent a letter to the city pleading to have the home spared and saved. What a story right? One of the great-grandkids just wrote a book about the whole story and I can't wait to read it.

"I'm going to ask the Packard family to be a part of the celebration when we save this old gal."

"I think that's a wonderful idea." I told Roxy.

When we left I dropped Roxy off at her place and headed home, I had about ten messages on my voicemail, Oliver and Martin, Jessica, Mrs. Green, Matt, Sara, Kiana, and even Sonya took time to call from her Mexican vacation. Martin left a message saying "Nikki, it's all over social media."

I took an ice pack from the freezer and put it on my cheek,

What a day!

ABOUT THE AUTHOR

M.A.Hansen

From a young age, M.A. Hansen has been writing short stories, poems, and novels for fun. This series is her first set of independently published books.
Her hobbies include reading mysteries, hiking, crocheting, and an infinite love of cooking and baking.
M.A. spends her time in the PNW and in sunny Southern California with her wonderful husband of 30 years. She is a mother and now a grandmother.

"I hope you enjoy reading about the adventure with my character Nikki Rodriguez, a journey of love, mystery, and laughs."
M.A. Hansen

The Amazing Nikki Rodriguez Series

Read them all and enjoy this fun and exciting mystery.

Start with Book 1

Crushes, Crimes and Cool Jazz

Beautiful lead singer Nikki Rodriguez sings like a pro with her band
Little Black Dress. Sexy and sultry her voice is true talent. Entertaining
the residents of sunny Rancho Niguel, California has been her job for
the last five years. All is fabulous and life is golden until a fellow
neighbor is found murdered in a fire in the sleek condo complex where
Nikki lives. Determined to find who committed this crime and
encouraged by her fellow friends and neighbors, she searches for clues
and teams up with the new handsome detective on the police force.
Love triangle that it is Nikki's ex the hottie fireman hasn't given up on
them yet, a game of cute flirting and close encounters make for
interesting whispers in the community. So between singing gigs, grande
lattes, relaxing yoga, and riding around in a red little convertible. Nikki
has a murderer on her back, a stalker sending her chilling text messages
and phone calls, a personal bodyguard, and a boss with a mysterious
past.
Can Nikki solve the crime and catch a killer before the next murder is
hers?

Book 2

Teammates, Terror and Thriller

It was a long hot summer, but now the leaves have turned brown, the temperature has cooled and Fall is bringing more than just Pumpkin Spice Lattes. It's October and Halloween is just around the corner in Rancho Niguel. Singer Nikki Rodriguez is in for more trouble when she finds the body of her old college swim teammate floating in a pool on a stormy day. Determined to find the one responsible Nikki is once again searching for clues and following leads. Along with the help of her old friends and her new boyfriend Detective Paul Anderson.
 Everyone in Rancho Niguel is ready for ghouls, witches, goblins, and vampires. Halloween is filled with tricks and treats and Nikki finds more than she bargained for.
 With the Halloween Harvest Festival and the Witches Brew Ball retirement party for Tank and Brinks, and who can forget Captain Matt Stevens who is still declaring his love for her, Nikki has her plate full. Yet all is not what it seems and soon secrets will be uncovered and hearts will be broken. One thing is true there's nothing scarier than trying to catch a killer.

Book 3

Weddings, Weapons and a White Christmas

Wedding Bells are in the air.

Diaz's wedding has finally arrived. As a favor, Nikki steps in as a bridesmaid for Lindsey after her cousin is called away to the Navy on an important mission. A wedding in December is always magic, especially when the location is at the ritziest hotel in Rancho Niguel, in the Grand Ballroom. Never a dull moment, at the same time a Guns and Amo convention is held in the banquet room next door, and soon a body is found in the parking lot.

Quickly Martin and Oliver become the prime suspects when stolen weapons are found in the art gallery. Does it have anything to do with the murder? Nikki investigates the case to clear their names and find a killer. Will Paul's ex-girlfriend become troublesome or will Nikki make her way back to Matt? Can all of this destroy the spirit of the holiday or will everyone end up with a White Christmas?

Book 4

Romance, Runaways and Rock n' Roll

Ah, the month of love! Valentine's Day is on its way! Tho, all is not

love in Rancho Niguel. When Matt's little sister runs away from home,

Nikki volunteers to help find her before she gets into trouble. The new

Youth Center is up and running but is someone trying to sabotage

Nikki's efforts? It's not all candy hearts and a box of chocolates, when

a local Rock n' Roll legend, turns up missing after a big concert. Can

Nikki find two missing persons, catch a vandal and keep her boyfriend

Paul away from his ex Stacie? It seems like only Cupid himself can

bring love to Rancho Niguel.